Jamie Stewart

PRICE MANOR: THE HOUSE THAT BLEEDS

The House That Bleeds: Book Two in the *Price Manor* series from Deadline Horror Collective. A horror novella.

First edition published February 2022 by Jamie Stewart in association with Deadline Horror Collective. Thank you for buying an authorised copy of this book.

TRADE PAPERBACK ISBN:

Edited by Jay Alexander.

delight at the treat before you. There is a moment in every reader's life where we stumble on an author whose words seem to *sing* right off the page and strike our story-hungry heart like a tuning fork. Many of us— Mr. Stewart included—felt that moment with our first Stephen King. (Mine? *Cell*. Not his best, yet still, the note struck true.) But I would argue that within the indie horror community, the author among us whose voice cuts through skin and muscle and tendon to that bloody knot of a heart inside the reader until every fiber of their being vibrates and sings back? That's Jamie Stewart.

Enter *The House That Bleeds*.

One thing I admire greatly about Jamie is his irrepressible joy for story. Here is an author who will never just recommend his own work, but who will champion other authors because he believes in their stories. He did this with Kelly Brocklehurst last summer when they co-edited the Blood Rites Horror anthology *Welcome to the Funhouse*. He and Kelly accepted, among others, a coming-of-age tale I'd written about an abandoned amusement park. But Jamie didn't stop there. He made sure everyone, myself included, knew about his love for this world I'd created. And when he and a group of talented authors began setting the foundation and laying the brick that would eventually become Price Manor, he approached me with an idea that might just bring their house and my park at odds. He came to me more than once, in fact, until he'd infected me with his sheer joy for story, and I saw what he saw, and I took his outstretched hand.

So let me return the favor now. Let me champion Jamie Stewart and his stories. Let me assure you that you hold in your hands one of the best haunted house tales I have ever had the pleasure of reading. A story suffused with gothic atmosphere and bursting with mystery and terror and suspense; betrayal and love and intrigue; danger that leaps off the page—*sings*—and grips you until the very end. Not since Shirley Jackson's *The Haunting of Hill House* have I seen such fully realized characters brought together in a strange house. Just as Jackson did with her character Eleanor, you feel for these hapless creatures as they stumble

PRICE MANOR
BOOK TWO
THE HOUSE THAT BLEEDS

A NOVELLA BY
JAMIE STEWART

DEADLINE

HORROR COLLECTIVE

FOREWORD **BY SPENCER HAMILTON**

Back for more? Welcome, welcome, welcome . . .

You hold in your hands, dear reader, the second installment in a bold new series: *Price Manor*, the story of a living, hungry, insatiable house and the victims it lures inside its walls from across time and space. If you read the first entry, *The House That Burns*, you may be wondering where our spooky friend Mike Salt has gone off to. But that's all just part of the magic and mystery of Price Manor—the authors that built this house are many and varied, and you never know which of us is going to turn up next to spin you a yarn.

Enter Jamie Stewart.

If you are somehow unfamiliar with Mr. Stewart, I can't help but squeal in giddy through the darkness of their own desires. You can't help but want the best for them—even as you fear the worst.

The House That Bleeds is, I believe, a masterpiece of horror. Jamie brings us through time and space in a way only Price Manor was supposed to, straight to the shores of Lake Silver in nineteenth-century Russia. And he doesn't let go, not even after we believe that Price Manor has.

But you can trust him. Mr. Stewart will guide you. It's your turn to take his outstretched hand. Just as it's his turn to lead you through those carved wooden doors of Price Manor.

Welcome. Come on in.

The house is waiting.

Spencer Hamilton
Author of *The Fear* and
Welcome to Smileyland

PART ONE

BLOOD AND SIN

CHAPTER **ONE**

1
OCTOBER 31ST, 1883
TULA, RUSSIA

It was October, but Alex could feel the bite of winter in the air. Although he was wrapped and gloved inside his thickest fur, its icy touch stabbed at the crinkled skin around his eyes, eyes that were still as blue as glacier water despite his sixty-four years. They stared at the abomination before him.

'Do you know what you're doing?' asked Baron Michael Volkov.

He sounded and looked mighty cheerful; there was a gleam of amusement in his beady eyes that Alexander knew all too well. The handsomeness may have ballooned from his face over the years as he gained fat, fat that had encroached further and further around those grey marbles he had for eyes, but Alexander could tell that the leader of their community was delightfully amused with himself.

You wouldn't know that I'd just put his wife into her grave a week ago, Alex thought. It was a thought that, while grim and bitter, caused a twitch of pain in what he had considered for some time to be his calloused heart. The pain was exquisitely sentimental and woeful. One look at the house, the house that shouldn't be, and the pockmarked, scarred tissue that he imagined caged that vital organ in his chest cocooned over it once more. It was an awful thing, the house, he thought, a nothing thing.

'Of course I don't know what I'm doing,' he replied, his voice irksome and gruff. 'This isn't something they teach you at seminar.'

'Well, you're all we've got, sorry excuse of a priest that you are,' said a third man. Tomac Ivanov's ancient voice was a rustic, reedy wheeze.

Alex sighed through gritted teeth; to unlock them would have allowed troublesome words to spew out. Tomac was the father-in-law to Michael Volkov, and former Baron of the lands. It was his wealth and position that Michael, having married into the family, now presided over. Another twinge of pain penetrated the rocky cavity of

Alex's heart as he thought of Michael's wife.

He was beginning to realise what a fool he must be for thinking that those feelings, which had bloomed in him as a boy, could ever have been bricked over. In some part of his person, he would forever be that young boy who had fallen heartedly and resolutely in love with Carla. It had been years, decades, since he had thought of himself as such, yet it was frightening how swiftly and strongly those feelings flooded back.

This time he pushed his feelings down on his own, which took considerably more effort without the grim sight of the house to help. It would not bode well for him to anger the men who had long ago orchestrated his fate with the help of the rest of Tula's high society: Heya Ivanov; Igor Morozov; Father Mikhail Goodwin. All dead now, all buried beneath Tula's rich soil. Yet the sense of loathing for each of them rose in him like bad indigestion burning his heart, his throat, the mind behind his eyes.

Not for the first time, he imagined wrapping his rough hands around the soft necks of those aristocrats, including the two still living before him, and squeezing until their eyes popped from their heads.

'On with you,' ordered Tomac from the back of his horse-drawn cart. He sat there on a seat of plush cushions, like an emperor on his throne, thumping his cane—made of a wood so dark that it was black, and crowned with a silver wolf's head for a handle.

'Let me remind you that I do not serve you. I serve the Lord, and through him this community,' Alex spat, in full view of everyone gathered on the shores of Lake Silver.

Despite his eighty-nine years making him the oldest member of their community, Tomac had the perfect answer for him. As the crowd uttered an audible gasp, he raised his trembling left arm—the one not clutching the cane—in a welcoming gesture while smiling ear-to-ear, and said, 'And it is the will of the community that you go inside and investigate this... occurrence. I only speak for them, as has been my role for the past fifty years.'

The smile that came from that wizened, yellowed skull was all dead, crooked teeth and gleeful malice. Alex understood from it that the man wanted him dead; that he had always wished so, because Alex was a thorn. No. Worse: an insect that could occasionally bite, and though his bite was no more than an annoyance to this man, it still meant he should be squashed. Alex supposed that if you woke up with such hateful motivations, there was a reason you'd survived to eighty-nine.

Alex's eyes slid over the faces of the hundred or so people clustered around him, seeing dark eyes under thick furs that they wore against the autumn chill, their breath like that of withering ghosts before them. He turned to the house.

It was unlike anything he had ever seen, its design alien to the harshness of the land Alex came from: a tall, thin spindle of wood, stone and glass that towered above them like a mighty spear. Its colour was a sooty navy. The waters of Lake Silver—still, on this windless day, gave it the look of a mirror that extended out to the horizon to merge with a sky made silver by the descending sun—pooled around the foundations of the house. The only section not lapped by water was a set of six stone steps leading to its entrance, a set of doors made of ornate wood and carved with numerous intricate lines.

For the first time, Alex recognised that this strange design looked old, as if it had been built some time long ago. This was not the case, and that was why he must go inside; the house had only come into being seven hours ago.

2

There is a road that points west along the shores of Lake Silver, used frequently by farmers to bring their tools into town. The lake, having no real edge to it on account of the surrounding fields being so flat, has always seemed to just... *begin*. The land around the circumference of the lake is boggy and thus unfit for building upon, which was why it came as such as surprise to Karl Fedorov to find, as he journeyed into town that morning, the house sitting there as if it had done so for uncountable years. This was especially surprising to him since he had come home along the very same road the night previous when returning from the tavern. His first instinct was to glance around, clutching the reins of his horse sharply, making sure that he was on the very same road that he thought himself to be.

Nursing a headache that lingered from his having spent the night before in his cups, he confirmed this place via the bleak, desolate space of muddy bogland stretching out around him, to be the same as it always was.

Yet, it was changed.

Changed by the spire that pointed at the vast, empty blue sky from the shoreline. He looked into the many windows of the house, seeing only the muddy fields reflected back, and felt nothing. It simply stood, defying the reality that he knew like a blankness in a person's memory.

Karl, who had spent many a night drunk, knew of such blankness. He tied the horse's reins to the wood of his cart and stepped down, boots squishing mud. 'Hello,' he called. His voice made his own shoulders flinch; it sounded so loud in the vast space.

Nothing stirred behind the windows, which stared out like eyes upon the land. His horse, Ruby, neighed beside him, also observing the sudden structure.

Karl called out again, stepping through the mud to the steps that rose up before the queer building. As with Alex, it was unlike anything he had ever seen before.

He was sure it was a house, but not a home like the farm he lived on. More like somewhere the Baron might live, although it looked nothing like the castle where he rested his head. What Karl struggled to mentally articulate was that the place had a grandness about   it.

He climbed the stone risers to the doors, which to him looked etched with the imagery of horses, wild ones like those he admired from afar when he hunted.

He went to knock upon the wood, but paused when he spotted a cord to the left that ran the height of the door and led to a bell made of dull iron. He yanked on the cord, causing the metal bell to produce a shrill toll that upset his ears. His shoulders flinched once more at its chime. Ruby neighed uneasily behind him.

When his ringing went unanswered Karl reached for the door handle, a knob of the same dull iron, yet despite his efforts it would not twist. Frustrated, head throbbing, he shouldered the two closed rectangles of wood, only to bounce off. Karl Fredorov stood six-foot four and weighed two hundred and ten pounds of solid farming muscle, yet neither door had given in the slightest.

Rubbing his shoulder, he stepped down, staring at the windows. Nothing. The house remained blank.

He thought about climbing to one of the low windows; these sat at the same height as the door, putting them ten feet off the ground. As he considered this, something cold lapped at his feet. Ruby neighed, a long, strained sound, and a crow cawed from the branches of a dead tree, its wood petrified white.

Karl glanced down to see a stream of red was pouring out from underneath the doors of the house. His nose filled with the metallic smell of it; having butchered enough animals, he knew it instantly. Blood.

The house was bleeding.

A yelp escaped Karl as he leapt back without thought, his feet scraping the edge of the top step, falling backward as the river of blood surged toward him. Suddenly he was in the air, weightless, then he slammed into the cold, wet muck.

Karl scuttled back on his elbows and heels, expecting to see the red river cascading over each of the risers. There was none. Not only was there no longer any blood pouring, but the stone was as clean as if it had never been there. Hyperventilating, Karl clawed his way to his feet, dashing to the cart where Ruby stamped her front left foot, making high keening sounds. His mind was alight with the thought that he needed to tell someone, anyone about the new house by Lake Silver, the one that seemed to have sprung out of nothing overnight.

'Well, are you going, or do we need to contact the church and request a new priest?' asked Tomac.

'I am,' growled Alex. He took one step, then another. Then another.

Lights flicked on in the windows of the house, bathing the shore in narrow slats of soft, ochre illumination. Alex paused in alarm, his mind a whirl as he peered up at the looming house. The light was not the flickering of flames found in the fireplaces and candles that he knew; it did not wither and dance, but held steady.

A cry of fear rang out from the crowd at the suddenness of the light. Alex looked to them and looked back at the house. It did look evil now, although none of its features had changed. Before, it had sat with an air of vacancy, like it wasn't really there.

Now it was alive.

Worse, Alex got a feeling that whatever dwelled within, whatever occupied the rooms made by its walls, wanted him to come inside. He looked over the many lit windows and saw Michael's piglet eyes alight with cruel amusement. There was something else: a sense of challenge.

It was this feeling that unlocked his body to him once more. He strode forward without a glance back, mounting the stone steps and seizing the iron doorknob, noting that the elegant designs on the doors were wolves with bared teeth. Where Karl Fredorov had found resistance Alex found none, twisting the knob with ease. He slipped into that dark chamber beyond, the door closing softly behind.

From the shore, each one of the villagers, except for those hard of hearing, heard the distinct click of a lock.

CHAPTER **TWO**

3

It wasn't until the door had clicked shut that Alex realised that, despite the light the house showed in its windows, the place he had entered was pitch black. He could not see a thing. As in other such times he grew aware of the vastness of his surroundings, his other senses alerting him to walls that existed several feet from him.

Out of the darkness he heard a sound. Someone was crying: a child. As to their gender he couldn't discern; they were too far away.

Alex cleared his throat to call out, clutching the silver crucifix that he wore around his neck for strength, and the lights came on. They did this slowly, their ochre light spilling out from various points at head height on either side of him, increasing in brightness until all the dark was dispelled.

'Hello,' Alex called out in the firmest voice he could muster, 'is anyone there?' No answer came back. Nor did the crying repeat.

The hall before him was empty of life. It was a grand, spacious area where the polished floorboards gleamed—their wood a rich, dark brown—around the sides of plush, scarlet rugs with ribbons of gold snaking through. As his eyes trailed round, he thought that he had never seen such fancy. The walls were papered with a navy so dark it was almost black. Weaving through it were silver vines that ended in leaves the colour of merle, depicting a forest scene. Every so often he spotted an image of a wild beast: a stag with a crown of bone; a bear on its hind legs; a fox sitting obediently. All silver, all staring hard from the walls on either side of him. Their eyes were like dull stars.

'Who's entered my wood?' he imagined them saying.

There were three passages leading off from the hallway. The one to the left led to a dining area, complete with a long table of more rich wood, lighter than that of the floor. Ten chairs encircled it. A grand fireplace, its flames crackling over coals and kindling, was carved into the wall behind. There was another fireplace, also lit, in the room to his right, a study with walls lined with bookshelves and comfortable seats of a type he'd never be able to afford. Both mantelpieces had the word *PRICE* carved into their fine wood.

Other than the noise of the fires, the only sound Alex could hear was the ticking of the grandfather clock against the wall to his right. Its golden pendulum swung languidly back and forth.

Alex took a step forward, causing the floor to creak underfoot, peering into both rooms. This was easy, as neither rooms had doors; instead, their entrances were archways built into the walls.

'My name is Alexander Nicholai. I am a priest from Tula. I mean no harm.'

As he said this, a volley of heavy, prodding footfalls rang out overhead. Alex's head jerked on his neck like a bird's, his blue eyes wild in his face at the suddenness of the sound. Dust floated down from the high ceiling, disturbed by the presence.

Pull yourself together, he scolded his hammering heart. You're a man of God, not an old maid.

Then another voice spoke up inside him, one that Alex had become increasingly more intimate with over the years, though never more so than in the last week.

Is that really true anymore? it asked, with a despairing type of clarity.

He already knew the answer. It was *no*. It had come to him only two nights before, alone in the shadows of his church, tears streaming salt trails down his craggy features as he lifted the bottle of vodka again and again to his lips. Trying to drown out the memories of Carla Volkov, whose heart-shaped face and raven-black hair flickered through his mind the way the cards in Karl Fredorov's hands sometimes did down at the tavern, their pictures a shimmering blur of movement. In his youth she had haunted him like a fever dream; now she was a ghost, cold and forever distant.

While Alex believed in God, his heart burned with a fury at the course of his life. It had become a kiln where hate, rage, regret and sorrow were hammered out over the flaming coals.

Yet Alex did not move to leave the house, breathing in air that smelt of varnish and dust. He had discovered long ago that there was another facet to his position as a priest than that of preaching God's ideas, a much more human responsibility, and that was being of service to the village he called his home.

Being here was just another part of his job, in the same way that being there for someone in grief or distress was. Sometimes he begrudged such tasks; in others he found a great degree of fulfilment in them. It was a job, and in exchange for it he held a respected position in the community that he had grown to appreciate, despite the animosity he had towards several of its members. So, he strode forward.

To do anything else would see Michael usurp him.

Alex realised he was wrong about his original assessment: there wasn't just one passageway ahead, but several. The one directly before him had walls that were all wood panelling as rich and polished as the floorboards; from these walls, corridors branched off diagonally in either direction so that a person could follow them round and move deeper into the bottom floor. Both of these corridors were narrow and draped in a bluish gloom, making him reluctant to try them; he chose to follow the light.

'Is there anybody home?' he said, stepping through the archway.

The walls of that titanic space echoed his words back to him. Surely this must be the heart of the house, he thought.

The room before him was a vast hexagonal shape with four archways leading in or out in the directions of all four points of a compass. A wide, carpeted staircase with an ornate banister of red wood climbed the walls in a spiral. His gaze followed it, drawn upward to the stained glass window that roofed the place, sunlight bleeding through in many vivid colours, showering down royal blue, evergreen, indigo and ruby. The image encapsulated in the glass above was that of a hunter - a nobleman, judging by his exquisite armour and cape, atop a white horse that was also draped in expensive cloths. Both the hunter and the animal stared down at Alex impassively.

'What is this place?' he heard himself mutter, his mouth hanging ajar.

Alex glanced around the four walls of the room, his mind buzzing with knowledge, his black robes fanning out as he twisted his upper half. It's impossible, he thought, yet his mind told him that the house he had seen outside could not possibly contain rooms of such size. I should be out on the lake now, he thought.

But he wasn't.

He suspected he was right in the centre of the house, yet the front door was more than seventy feet behind him. The house's exterior had been that of a tall, thin spindle of a building, perhaps only fifty feet of length by forty. Its insides were far more vast.

'I contain multitudes,' he whispered, his voice a croak.

Alex blinked, frown lines creasing his forehead. He had no idea why he had said such a thing, and upon trying to recapture the reasoning his mind offered nothing.

Shaking his head, he wandered over to the base of the grand staircase. The footfalls he'd heard had come from upstairs; some sort of devilry was here, and he intended to seek it out. After all, that was his job in a manner. It was a bitter thought in the light of recent events, but Alex climbed onward anyway.

The staircase wound around the circumference of the room, illuminated by the same strange, steady lights that he had already seen. Alex tried to examine one of them, remarking on the finery of the glass bulb that contained the light, but unable to discern its alchemy. He turned his attention to the walls, which were coated in the same navy paper—with its twisting silver vines—as the front hall. Only there were no animals in these woods, it seemed, and each vine ended not in a merle leaf, but a bright, red rose, their flowers in bloom. They were of such a vivid colour that he felt compelled to touch them, thinking that they would be painted on. To his surprise he discovered that they were indeed cloth, their individual threads as soft as silk under his calloused fingers. He stood for some time, his index finger stroking the lovely scarlet thread, his mouth filling with saliva, filling, filling, filling. Then he swallowed. It filled again... filled with each smooth stroke of his fingers. At some point he became satisfied and, on returning his hand to his side, mouth still feeling overly full, discovered he was on the third-floor landing, the highest point of the staircase. The corridor beyond was not as brightly lit as the hexagonal stairwell with its stained-glass roof; the lights that adorned its walls seemed to project only a fraction of the illumination of those he had already encountered, leaving the corridor in semi-shadow. He thought about descending to the second floor, sure that the footfalls he had heard came from that level, but a degree of sluggishness had descended over him that he was forced to shake his head against. With plodding feet, knuckling at eyes which felt sleep-crusted, Alex entered the corridor and left the staircase behind.

The corridor was narrow compared to the grandeur he had experienced already; still, Alex could walk down it with both his arms held out and be unable to touch the walls. This produced a giggle from him as he slapped them back to his sides, then clapped his palms together, producing sharp smacking sounds.

'Come out, come out,' he mused, his sluggishness having teetered into a drunkenness.

The same navy walls with silver coils followed him on either side. He could only make these out in the sections directly beneath the lamplight, the rest hidden in the corridor's gloom. From what he could see in these parts, there were hunters on horseback in the woods now; hunters like the one in the glass roof, blood red capes trailing behind them as they gave chase with spears and swords in their hands.

To look at them was to hear the sound of horses neighing, the thunder of many hooves, the clatter of armoured bodies and even gruff, eager voices. They were faint sounds, almost out of earshot as he took turn after turn after turn down gloomy passages lined with doors that he felt no need to try.

'I'm going to get you,' he sang, imagining himself as part of the hunting party.

He was running now, his legs making great loping, shambling strides, his boots thumping the carpet. The hunt on the walls was a cacophony in his ears, the sound of galloping hooves that of a stampede whipping through the undergrowth of a forest that wasn't green, but midnight blue. Alex's arms were pistons at his sides, fingers open, twitching like claws, as he rounded corner after corner.

A jangling part of his person, a forgotten part, bounced into his right hand. It was his crucifix, the metal hot in his palm.

He stared at it, legs still pumping beneath him, without hearing the pursuit anymore. What were they pursuing, anyway? He looked up just in time to see that he was racing into a dead end with no time to stop.

Alex managed to get an arm up, but still he thudded to a halt at full speed, his nose becoming a sharp spike of pain as he folded backward to the floor. Tears welled in his eyes, blurring his vision of the dark place he was in. Groaning, he touched the bridge of his nose with a finger and a thumb only to feel that sharp stab once more.

Alex rolled on his side and spat out a glob of blood. There was a sludge of it at the back of his throat, filling his mouth with its iron taste. He had tasted the same on the staircase before, when he had stared dreamily and stroked the soft, scarlet fibres of a rose on the wall.

What was I doing? he thought, rubbing at his aching brow. His head felt hungover.

Spitting again, he observed a peculiar sight: the swiftness of his blood soaking into the carpet. It was as if something underneath was sucking, draining his blood through the fur of the carpet, leaving no stain behind.

He lay, his muscles locked as the heat in them turned to cold, his body no longer coated in beads of sweat but what felt like ice. His skin crawled as the realisation dawned on him that he was in trouble. And the house stood silent, a tomb around him, as this thought worked its way through his mind.

The house was evil; of that, he was certain. If not evil in itself, then whatever malignant force had conjured it was. Before he had walked its halls, feeling the awkwardness of being an intruder. Now he felt like an animal in a trap.

He had been stupid, careless. And that made him angry.

Alex lurched to his feet, chest heaving as his rage boiled over from the kiln that was his heart.

'What the hell is going on here?!' he yelled into the dimly lit passage.

No response. At least, nothing from the corridor that stretched out before him with its feeble light fixtures before shooting left.

A glance to his right, however, caused him to flinch away from the wall. The image within the silver wood showed a troop of horse-backed hunters, their armour gleaming merle, their unfurled capes a bright crimson, staring right at him. One of them, the leader, sat at the head of the group, his eyes onyx black. The right eye winked at Alex.

Who were the hunters on the wall

hunting?

Footsteps, loud and prodding, thumped from somewhere nearby.

'Now what is this new madness?' he said.

Ensuring his crucifix was clutched tight, Alex took off at a jog. It was clear to him that it had brought him out of the house's enchantment; it seemed God still had some faith in him, despite his wretched heart.

He flew down the corridor's every twist and bend, gaining on the thumping steps to the point where he chased a shadow on the walls, but never further. Every time he launched around another turn, expecting to see whatever or whomever this shadow was tethered to, the distance between them had grown. Each time he managed to gain on it he was able to hear the thing's breathing, for no human should breathe like that; it was a piggish, guttural honking sort of noise.

Alex didn't know what he would do once he came upon the creature that produced that sound, or if he even wanted to. The crucifix, so hot in his hand that he was surprised it wasn't melting, urged him on.

The chase ended as the corridor widened out before another set of stairs. These were nowhere near as grand as those in the hexagonal room, more of a cross between a staircase and a ladder ascending into a rectangular recess in the ceiling. Beyond its frame was darkness.

Whatever he was chasing had gone up there. The crucifix throbbed in his hand with a giddy pulse; still he paused at the foot of the staircase and stared upward into the shadows. They gave away no secrets.

The house was silent all around him, holding its breath. Its air no longer smelt of polish and cleanliness, but the spice of dust and of things starting to grow damp.

Alex gripped the sides of the staircase, its wood rough beneath his calloused hands. Despite being sixty-four and the village priest he still kept in shape, helping out his flock when it came to harvest time, toiling in the fields with them from sunup to sunset. While he'd never wanted that life for himself, he actually enjoyed the work: the way his muscles ached and how the people embraced him, including at the tavern for a drink after it was done.

This was just like that, he told himself. Just another part of the job.

He began the climb, the steps creaking beneath his weight as his heartbeat pounded in his ears. The crucifix grew calmer with each step, less like a throbbing pulse and more an inanimate object heated by his hand.

At the last rung on the ladder Alex paused, gazing up into the darkness, unable to see any more than he had on the bottom step. He became aware of his breathing now, how jagged and quick it was. How it filled his mouth with the taste of the fish pie that he'd had for lunch: delicious then, rank now. His lips felt chapped and dry; licking them, he reached with his left hand and pulled his head up through the hole in the ceiling and into the void.

Though his eyes could not penetrate the darkness, Alex got a sense that the space around him was cramped. He dared not stand upright, instead clutching the frame of the attic with his head hunched, aware that whatever he had followed here could be waiting to spring upon him now.

With his left hand he fumbled in his robes, his eyes never leaving the veil of darkness, and retrieved a matchbox from his pocket. In trying to open the box, he spilled it in its entirety onto the wooden slats of the attic floor. Still he was unable to take his eyes off the darkness, afraid that doing so would lead whatever hid in it to seize its chance and attack. Finally, his sweat-greased fingers snatched upon one of the thin sticks of wood.

Alex scratched it against his nail, a habit of his, and its end flared into flame. It didn't illuminate much, but its flickering glow pushed back a limited amount of darkness to reveal the outline of something round straight in front of him. His breath was once more dry and rank as he extended his arm into the gloom.

The orange light of the match pooled and rippled across the features of a grotesque deformity. It was a person, only its head was three times the size of any normal human being's head. Its skin was of a whiteness that suggested it had never seen the sun, its left side sagging noticeably lower than the right to give the impression of dough or some sort of plaster rather than flesh. The eye on that side was a swollen slit; the other was a vast, grey orb that stared with glee. Wisps of lank, grey hair framed the creature's face. A string of drool hung down from a mouth lined with tombstone-black teeth. However, its horrendous appearance was not the reason Alex felt like a fist had punched into his chest to squeeze his heart; it was the vague similarity in its distorted features to those of the woman he loved, Carla Volkov, that did. The thing opposite him sighed one word: 'Boo.'

On the air of its breath, his match blew out.

CHAPTER **THREE**

1

Alex screamed as the thing clambered over the attic boards towards him, the dark suddenly filled with the creature's grunting breath. He flinched back as a long stalk-like arm as grey as corpse meat slashed out in front of his eyes. The wind of it, foul and putrid, swept by and made him gag as the thing's ragged nails raked the air.

He lurched out of the way—just.

Fright lit in him as his upper body swung backward. Too far. His boots slipped on the step at the moment the ladder collapsed on itself, becoming a slide. The wood that had been so rough was now as smooth as ice and he slid, smacking his collar on the lip of the attic.

Crying out, he watched a section of the carpeted floor below fold back like a trapdoor into a dark void. Snapping his head up, he saw his attacker leap onto the slide, her grey eye shining like a foul lantern as the house swallowed him into darkness.

He plunged through what he could only assume were the innards of the house, using his palms to propel him from the pursuing monster. It seemed to work; the wind of her claws scraping at his neck faded. Still, every time he threw his head up, he saw that phantom light of her eye, unwinking and sour. His only reference to her in the pitch black.

When he eventually shot out into light, it was into open air. Alex just had the time to register that he was looking down into a room from a bird's eye view, then he was tumbling toward the floor, a red carpet snaked with gold.

For the second time that evening, Alex collided against a solid surface. A plume of dust erupted from the carpet that he flopped onto, choking him. Coughing, he rolled over, expecting to see the horrible creature with the elongated limbs falling upon him, but he only saw the square section of the ceiling that he'd come through swing shut. Once it did, he couldn't make out any seam or edge in the plaster above, like the trapdoor didn't exist at all.

Swaying, pain wracking his body—particularly his arms, which he'd used to cushion his fall—Alex stood. He was in what appeared to be a library, a vast rectangle of a room lined with bookshelves. A giant fireplace at one end was framed between two narrow windows. A pair of double doors were shut at the other end of the room. A gale was storming outside the windows, pelting the glass with water from the lake.

The room swayed against it like a ship at sea, its floorboards a chorus of creaks. He felt each dip and rise through his feet and thought: what now? What else has this twisted place got in store for me? Alex was beginning to regard the place not as an *it*, but as something *alive*. Its presence assured him of such.

Plunging through the darkness had felt like being inside the bowels of some titanic monster. His ears had filled with the scream of wood and the clap of brick as the house seemed to rearrange itself, creating the pathway of the slide as he fell through it. Even now he could feel it watching him with many eyes unseen.

It had ejected him into this room; why?

He needed to get out, he knew that much. Whatever powers were invested in him as Tula's religious leader were not enough. Whether that was because of his own conflicting feelings towards his belief, or because the house was too powerful, he did not know. The truth was that he did not know enough about it; perhaps if he had some knowledge of whatever haunted this accursed place, he would be better equipped to battle it. As it was, he felt like a plaything to it, a toy in some shrieking child's hand that they would break once they'd bored of it.

Alex stalked towards the windows, figuring he could break the glass and flee that way if they were low enough. However, rubbing the dirty grime from one of the panels revealed that he was some thirty feet off the ground. He could see the flat shoreline of Lake Silver, as bleak and desolate as always. There were no people around, either because they had gone, or because of the angle from which he was viewing the lake.

Wind lashed the glass, throwing water so hard it hit like hail. Strange: Alex could smell sea salt, which was impossible as Lake Silver was formed of fresh water from the mountains. Still, he could smell it, and once more he could hear a steady *drip-drip-drip* from somewhere nearby.

A glance around alerted him to the condition of the room. While he had smelt damp on the third storey, he had seen no obvious signs of it. The library reeked of it. The dark wood of its bookshelves was disintegrating with grey-black mould. Its carpets were faded and threadbare. The books themselves looked waterlogged, their leather covers bloated, their pages on inspection like seaweed.

Alex moved to the fireplace, his eyes scanning the names on mottled spines; names like SALT, ELIOT, NEWLIN, GOODWIN, GLOOM, ALEXANDER and HAMILTON. Names by authors he had never heard of before. Their works must surely be occult in nature to be inside such a place, he thought.

The dripping noise was louder by the cold fireplace. Like the mantelpieces he had already seen, this one had the name *PRICE* carved into the wood. Alex ran his index finger along the grooves of the words; the wood was spongy to the touch.

A mirror presided over the fireplace, ringed in a golden frame, its silver surface dirtied by black mould. He looked at his own reflection, at the haggard face, the white beard that he kept neat as a continuation of his jaw, the black caterpillar eyebrows. Something moved in the depths of the mirror.

Alex spun, his blue eyes darting across the room, but there was no one there. The *drip-drip* noise had increased to a steady patter from inside the fireplace.

When he returned his gaze to the mirror, he observed to his horror the shadow of what he assumed was a man step toward its surface and hammer upon it with a fist.

'Get out!'

The voice was muffed, distorted, as if speaking through water. The mirror's surface vibrated in its golden frame with the force of the blow.

Alex staggered backward, wondering what new horror this was. Even now he could feel the gaze of the room upon him; his skin prickled as if with a thousand hostile wasp strings. The house no longer felt playful; its very air, thick with the mould that crawled at the back of his throat, felt hot with anger.

The pattering sound had become a gushing from within the chimney.

Alex observed with widening eyes as a torrent of blood, so dark it was almost black, jetted down onto the base of the fireplace, splashing the soot-crusted brick around it.

The shadow on the other side of the mirror hammered against it once more.

'RUN!'

Alex obeyed, spinning and launching into a sprint for the exit. Behind him, the blood had stopped being a jet and progressed into a flood. On throwing a glance over his shoulder he witnessed a waterfall of it surge down the chimney and explode against the fireplace brick, forming a wave that rushed outward, drowning everything in crimson.

Turning back, Alex noticed he was no closer to the door. His calves gave a yell of exhaustion as he became aware that the room had shifted, that he was now running on an inclined slope, that the double doors were now higher. Another glance behind him showed him that the room seemed to exist like a child's seesaw; the blood, now a massive pool, had collected in the bottom corner. The fireplace was submerged and blood covered half of the windows and bookshelves on that side, its weight causing the entire room to rear up.

Alex was running at a slant now, trying to avoid spilling into the blood, his lungs hitching for breath. Already, he knew it was too late. Suddenly, he was using his hands to clutch at the ruined carpeted floor for purchase. Chunks of it tore off as his feet lost their grip. Collapsing forward, he slid down the length of the room toward the blood pool, aware that his calves were sighing with relief.

The diseased liquid struck him like a wet fist.

Despite trying to keep his mouth closed, it punched through his lips and flowed over his gums. It tasted how he imagined rusted iron must taste. His skin squirmed as it flowed over him, pulled by unknown currents, blind, deaf, speechless, breathless. He fought against the tide, shambled, floundered in the red ichor, yet no matter how much he cycled his limbs he remained trapped beneath the flood.

CHAPTER **FOUR**

He was dying. His strength was fading; he could feel it being sapped out of his limbs as he continued to flail uselessly, his lungs aflame inside him. A current was pulling him now, and he tumbled through the red murk.

Wherever it was taking him, his head broke the surface first. Gasping for air, he was aware of spewing forth into a new darker space, carried by the red tide. One second he was floating in its stream; the next, he was thrown on his hands and knees onto a stone floor as blood gushed around him. The volume of it spilling from what he observed was another trapdoor above roared in his ears.

Alex was hardly concerned with that, vomiting up blood and bile as his torso moved like an accordion to replenish his oxygen. By the time he had regained some level of normality, the last of the blood was soaking into the concrete floor without a trace.

Darkness surrounded him on all sides as he knelt, a dripping red figure in a cone of white light cast by an unseeable source above. A glance at his hands showed that they were caked in the viscous liquid.

'Why have you come here, red priest?' hissed a serpentine voice from the shadows.

Alex's head shot up. Before him, swaying out of the gloom like a drunk, was Carla Volkov.

It wasn't really her, nor was it the hunched, toad-like version he had seen in the attic. She was stretched, her body ten feet tall and fiendishly thin. There was a sickle of a smile on her lips; in the place of her teeth were fangs of silver metal that were both dull and shining at once. She swayed toward him in a rotten bridal dress, its yellowed cloth diaphanous and rustling with each step.

Alex glared at the sick, poisoned sight of the woman he loved, rage flaming bright in his heart and feeding new strength into his legs. If this is the end, he thought, then I'll end standing, and he rose to his feet. Arms at his sides, fingers hooked into claws, he intended to hurt this mocking creature before his death—death being the only outcome he could think of now, having experienced all he had within the house. Standing, teeth gritted, jaw set as the stretched creature floated into the light on bare feet, it felt like the end. Alex no longer sensed the watchful, toying presence of the house from his surroundings; instead it emitted from the thing before him like a beacon of insidious pleasure. The house, in this form, was loving this.

Alex vowed to make it regret that.

'Most of your ilk are offended by my being, they come here, men, all self-righteous or with something to prove, their chests puffed up, and I break them. I feast on them. But you're different. You wear the cloth, but your heart is a cauldron of hate.'

The stretched creature circled the circumference of the light like a stalking cat, never fully stepping inside. Alex followed its movements, always making sure he faced it head-on. Its voice slithered like the body of a snake, making the flesh of his shoulders tense.

'Lies!' spat Alex, clutching his blood-drenched crucifix.

'No, it is you who is lying now,' hissed the creature of the house, its tone mockingly gleeful. 'You have belief, but not faith, preacher. Your heart is at war with it. Holding that trinket will only get you so far without the faith to back it up.'

The stretched creature slashed out with one of its freakishly slender limbs, each finger ending in a needle-like nail the same metallic colour of her teeth. Those nails raked the crucifix from his hand, tossing it into the darkness.

Alex stared after it, horrified. He did not think of the power that had throbbed from it, but of his mother handing him the box that contained it the day he was due to leave Tula to join the priesthood. She had squeezed his hand, hard, as if ensuring that the event became marked in his memory; it had worked.

For the first time in forty-two years, he was without it.

'How do you know these things?' he asked, hearing terror in his own voice.

'I have ways of knowing, of seeing what lurks inside,' it replied, still circling, still stalking. 'There was a time when you saw your duty as spreading the word of your precious, insecure deity, but no longer, not since returning to Tula. In the darkest hours of the night, when you are alone and walled

60

inside that church of yours, when there's no one around to see your true feelings come out.'

The cone of light winked out, smothered by fog that solidified into the grey brick of his church, made silver by the moonlight shining through windows on high which was sliced and sectioned by the simple architecture of the building's curved ceiling so that it fell in blades of silver, allowing for shadows to remain between the rows of pews that rested on either side of him. The stretched creature stood in the distance, to the right of the dais and before the pulpit where he preached.

'This is the place; it is both your sanctuary and your hell.'

It hissed this while climbing the steps to his pulpit, stamping its feet on each one.

'This is where you REGALE your congregation with holy proclamations!' yelled the heinous thing, sweeping its slender limbs back like Christ on the Cross. Its voice boomed against the stone walls. 'All while they smile up at you.'

The pews, which had been empty, were suddenly full. Alex spun, seeing everyone he knew stare dreamily at the stretched creature. The colour had run out of them:

their bodies, their clothes, even their eyes were dust-grey like that which amassed on the high shelves of a bookcase. All were smiling. No, not just smiling, grinning to the point where their cheeks looked ready to tear.

He wandered between the rows, noticing that he was clean of blood; his robe was once more midnight black. His hands, his fingers; even where the blood had congealed and caked beneath his nails was gone. His boots, however, squeaked with each step, leaving bloody footprints on the white stone. Yet when he inspected the leather soles of each boot, he found them to be pristine as if new.

Seeing that trail of crimson behind him was like a gut-punch that expelled all the air from his lungs. He stared, hollowed out, and in place of all his fear came guilt.

'They smile at you because they all know the truth, and none smile more than these men.'

The stretched creature gestured with its needle-like nails to the front row. Sat there was Michael Volkov, big and bold, beside Tomac Ivanov, his ancient back forever hooked forward so he clutched at his cane with the wolfish head even as he sat on the pew. Both men were smiling so hard their gums were bleeding. Veins of running red snaked down their chins and dripped onto the white stone floor.

'The truth?' Alex asked the creature on high.

'Years ago, there were two young people in love,' said the creature.

Something akin to sunlight dawned in the tall, arched window behind the dais. To his surprise, Alex saw that the imagery of the Lord's divine light had disappeared; in its place, the stained glass had become a yellowed backdrop for two individuals, one male, one female. He had seen a shadow show before, where people used dark cut-outs to tell a story. The two figures looked like that, except they were moving.

The man seemed to hold out a flower to the woman, who accepted it.

With a pang of sorrow, Alex recognised the flower: a lily.

'Sadly, these two were shackled by the conventions of their time,' came the voice from his pulpit, as if reading from a fairy tale.

In the window the two figures were ripped apart by chains snaking into the scene from either side of the frame. Alex felt a similar chain coil around his heart.

'He was low-born, a farmer's son, destined to spend his life toiling outside. She was high born, doomed to live in silent servitude at the corner of every conversation: a pretty vase; nice to look at, but not something to expect much from. These were their bonds, in a place where such things are paths. Nobody suspected anyone would think of ever rising above them, except for two. One was a stranger, who claimed to have wealth but had none. The other was a father, who had wealth in his line but none at hand. Both conspired against the pair.'

The eldritch, golden light winked out, and with it the charcoal figures that had re-enacted Alex's early years before his bulging eyes. The windowpanes had returned to their original imagery, sapphire glass surrounding a white cloud raining a ray of transcendent light down upon a forested land. The chain around his heart squeezed.

'You know what happens next, though you didn't at the time.'

The stretched creature moved like a serpent, its elongated body coiling around the pulpit until it stood erect once more at his side. Its sickle-like smile had never looked more devilish. Alex thought it was enjoying this.

'At the time you were clueless. You knew only that a marriage proposal had been made, and that a young girl, out of naive loyalty to her kin, had accepted.'

The creature placed the palm of its left hand on his shoulder as if to give comfort.

'Do you want to tell the rest of the story?'

Alex refused to answer, his lips clamped shut. The creature glided around him, stood on his left side, holding onto his shoulders with both of its hands now.

'You uncovered it— it's why your people smile at you all those years later—having used that bright star of a mind to escape your place in life and then return back like some conquering hero, didn't you? I know you did. You thought you were going to serve them like Reverend Father Goodwin did in your day—and on the outside, you have persisted to fulfil that role, but your real duty became that of a historian.'

From the wooden floorboards beneath the dais a knocking sound erupted, causing Alex to stumble back.

'Ahh… here it is. A collection of sins.'

The creature flung the dais aside as if it

was nothing; it shattered against the wall of the church. Bending at the knees it pried the floorboards apart, inserting its needle-like nails between them and wedging them up. This done, it scooped out a black leather-bound book that Alex knew all too well from the unrevealed cavity.

'The truth, all that befell Tula after your escape. The secret proposal from a father to a stranger, offering his daughter's hand in marriage in exchange for *murder*… and all the evil since. The recorded trajectory of the blight you helped to unleash on this land.'

'What are talking about?' gasped Alex. 'I had nothing to do with what they did.'

Yet even as he gestured at Michael and Tomac, that sense of guilt swelled inside him, filling his flesh with a panicking heat. He stared as the creature grinned its sickle-steel grin down at him in the silver moonlight, sweat rolling into his eyes.

'Come now. You considered yourself to be a robbed man, wounded and betrayed. And you are, but you are also responsible.'

'How am I responsible?' he said, knowing the answer, fearing it.

'There was a time—was there not?—when you had the opportunity to say something to

Luka Ivanov, the Good Baron, before a young Tomac Ivanov took his place. Something that could have made a difference. Yet you were afraid.'

'It wasn't my place, you don't just...' snapped Alex weakly.

'Only children make excuses, Alexander Nicholai.'

It said this with gleeful relish; its lips, a mess of white scars luminous in the moonlight, pulled back over its grey gums. The leather book lay open in its hands, its pages making the sound that only paper can make as it's spooled through.

'The Good Baron would have listened, you know; even at the time, you knew that in your heart. You were just too scared, too bound by the chains of your station. And all that has happened was allowed to pass: tax increases, land seizures, death.

'Tell me what happened to your family's farm?'

'Shut up,' muttered Alex, backing away on legs that had no strength. To his horror, he saw he was still leaving bloody footprints.

'You failed them; you used that bright star of a mind and fled like a whipped puppy. It's an excuse.'

'Shut up,' Alex said with more force. His voice echoed off the stone.

The grey congregation were staring at him now, their smiling heads following his retracing steps.

'Worst of all, you failed *her*,' hissed the stretched thing. 'And there was no excuse then. You came back, you saw what years of living under these men's thumbs had done to her, your great love, and did nothing.'

'What was I supposed to do?' screamed Alex, tears in his eyes.

The church was gone: the moonlight, the congregation, all of it. Alex found himself in the first hallway he had stepped into, its strange light fixtures producing that steady, ochre light as the gold pendulum within the grandfather clock swung, ticking away the seconds. There was no stretched creature in front of him, just the double doors that he had entered through.

On seeing them he lunged forward, the tail of his robe billowing out behind him as he grasped a door handle and yanked. The door came away so fast that its lock didn't have the chance to fully leave the socket, causing the whole thing to judder as he ripped it wide. He darted down the steps and was met not with the cold squelch of mud.

It was stone; his boots clapped on it as he halted.

Alex looked up to find he was not on the pancake-flat shore of Lake Silver, nor were the villagers collected before him waiting on his return. The tree was there, the same white, petrified wood with its fan of dead branches; only it was rooted not in earth, but on the edge of a mighty drop.

In the distance beyond, nestled between two valleys carpeted with pine trees, was Tula.

'What the fuck is happening?' said Alex.

CHAPTER **FIVE**

Alex had lived long enough in Tula to know where he was in its surrounding landscape by his view of the town. Seeing Lake Silver off to his left, he knew that the mountain he was on belonged to a range south of the town. The fact that the house had moved somehow during his time inside was forgotten the moment he identified that something was different about Tula.

He didn't know what it was at first, peering over the precipice as the wind clawed its way up the rock, whipping his robes. Then, with a gasp, it clicked in his brain.

The church tower was wrong. It had been damaged. Alex's eyesight was good, yet he had to squint to make out sense out of what he was seeing. It wasn't damaged; the church tower looked... incomplete.

It looked...

Alex Nicholai turned ever so slowly on his heel. The house sat, its thin, three-storey design, unlike anything he had known, seemingly moulded with the pewter rock of the mountain that rose up in jagged towers.

'What have you done?' he whispered into the cool air.

The wind was like a balm for his body, which had grown feverish once more. The house never moved; its windows, its navy boards, soot-black brick and tiles gave away nothing of the madness inside. Yet it wasn't innocent; that cruel, teasing presence radiated off of it, nudging him to go on down the mountain into the town.

Alex blinked as his mind registered another fact. He had entered the house in October; the air at this height was much too warm for that time of year, and instead it felt more like July. He twisted, turning back to the view from the cliff.

Yes, it was summer. July, he guessed from the vivid yellow of the farming fields—and, lo and behold, wasn't that someone working on his fathers' farm amongst all that colour? There was, although his family's farm had been seized by Michael Volkov in 1863. The year that the bell tower of his church was completed.

His fever turned to panic in that instant. Unable to help himself Alex took off into a sprint, following a curved path in the rock that led to the valley forest. There, it merged with a trail that he recognised as the eastern road. By the time it had bought him to town he could only manage a brisk march, his legs as stiff as tree trunks, both throbbing with individual pains, his body slick with sweat.

On the outskirts of his father's farm, his right leg went into spasm. A yell escaped him as he fought to stay standing, the dust of the lane drying his nose as he hyperventilated. He managed it, his upper torso going ramrod straight while his fingers flexed and relaxed, flexed and relaxed, until the spasms ceased.

The muscles of his right leg were locked, useless. He had to drag himself to the nearest fence post, trailing a furrow in the dust from it.

'Goddamnit,' he seethed through gritted teeth.

Alex leaned on the fence post, lifting his stiff leg off the ground and trying to rotate his foot in the hopes that it would encourage the other muscles to loosen. His attention diverted; he didn't notice the figure in the field until the pain began to ease.

Looking up, he spotted the man right away, even though there was still some distance between them, enough that the sun's severe yellow light made his features indistinguishable and his eyes water. Alex knew who he was. He knew by the thick mop of reddish-brown hair on his head, a darker hue to that which his own had been before the colour leaked out of it. He recognised his signature clothes, the brown waistcoat, the white shirt and brown trousers; Alexei Nicholai had worn them every day of his life, or at least in his son's memories he seemed to.

The man working was his father; he held onto the reins of a horse behind him, guiding it as it pulled a plough that churned up potatoes from their earthen beds into the light. Coming up behind him over the crest of a hill was another figure, younger, familiar, his hair a mix of his mother's blonde and his father's darkness. A string of other boys followed him, all with wicker baskets hanging from their necks by slings of fabric.

Tears wormed down Alex's cheeks as he

watched what his brain said must be a mirage but couldn't have been. He watched his father continue to lead the horse—whose name was Luna, if Alex's memory served him right—as the boys, including a teenaged version of himself, dipped and rose, picking the newly freed potatoes from the soil.

Alex had no memory of seeing a stranger in black observing them work, an old man to his young eyes, but that didn't mean there hadn't been one. He had, however, plenty of memories of performing this gruelling task, and in watching it he could feel the weight of the basket upon his neck, the rough slings drinking the sweat off his skin, the ache that began in his lower back and gradually intensified until his muscles felt like steel that'd been beaten out of shape, and always the glare of the sun beating upon them as they marched. He had loathed that work back then, yet at the end of each day when the sun had sunk below the horizon his father would wordlessly thank him with a few pats on the back that seemed to make it all worth it. Alexei Nicholai seemed to communicate with that one gesture that he knew exactly what his son was feeling—felt it too—and that he was thankful that his son had endured it without complaint even though he'd wanted to. He felt ashamed for having felt as he did, but also proud and sad that his father had to live such a life.

If my father and I are here, asked a part of his mind, then who else is?

'Spot of trouble, my friend?' asked a voice to his left.

It was a friendly voice, one he recognised though he had not heard it in over forty-two years. Turning his head Alex discovered that Father Mikhail Goodwin was staring at him, his figure just about contained by his chocolate-coloured robes.

The last Alex had heard of Father Goodwin was that his body had been found in a river hundred miles outside of Tula with his throat slit. Rumours had abounded that as the years went on the drink had gotten to him, in so far as to mean that the more he drank, the more he talked about town secrets that were better kept that way. Not that the people hadn't already suspected what he said; just that the town leadership preferred such theories to remain as suspicions, rather than become gossip at the tavern.

And they had succeeded.

All Alex had been able to find out when he

had taken over Goodwin's position was that he had talked; no one would tell him what it was that he had actually talked *about*.

He supposed he should feel sorry for the father, seeing him now, his white beard unkempt and somehow greasy looking, his cheeks ruddy with drink already, but he didn't. There was a sharpness to his slate-grey eyes that Alex had never noticed in his youth; everything about his jolly appearance sucked him in, made him relax his guard, because what harm could that rosy-apple face cause? His eyes told a different story; they reminded him of the windows of the house, gazing at him with cruel interest.

'And a stranger, too,' exclaimed Goodwin, before Alex could reply. He must have seen something in Alex's face too, because he added, 'You'll find that everyone knows every face in these parts. Have you injured yourself, my man?'

Alex glanced down at his leg, which he was still holding off the ground. 'Just a cramp is all,' he replied, feigning good cheer.

'Oh good,' cried the father, 'and what brings you to Tula, may I ask? Are you a companion of the young Volkov boy?'

A hardness entered Alex's face as all the

heat seemed to vanish from the day. The breeze continued to sigh through the fields, ever flowing seas of green, no longer offering any relief from the sun's heat; instead, he shivered against the fence post.

'What boy would that be?'

'I haven't had the pleasure to meet him yet,' Goodwin answered. 'Story is that he's from more modern places—Saint Petersburg, I believe. Come looking to make his mark on the world. I take it you are not companions?'

Alex didn't answer; he could only stare at the doomed man, his mind awhirl.

'What the hell did you do?' bellowed Alex as he limped into the house, his body an agony of throbbing knots from the path up the mountain.

The doors, which he had batted open, clapped against the walls. The house, or whatever presence inhabited it, did not react. The front hall was as he had left it, with the ornate grandfather clock tolling away time underneath the soft hue of the inexplicable lights. The fireplaces in nearby rooms crackled; again, just as he had left them.

Or so he thought at first.

As he began to regain his haggard breath, he heard the clink of metal. It was coming from the dining room on the left. Alex leaned his upper body forward, peering through the oval entrance with its plush wooden trim, and saw that Carla was setting the table for two.

This was not the stretched-out creature that had conversed with him before, nor was it the toad thing that had chased him through the wall cavities of the house. This was not the Carla Volkov that he knew, either, but the Carla Ivanov he had known as a young man. Her hair was not lank seaweed but thick and vibrant, the colour of a crow's wing. It fell in black waves on either side of her heart-shaped face, where her cheeks were chubby bubbles above dimples that grew more pronounced the more her pink lips smiled.

He remembered those lips, their taste and touch, the sweet musk of her hair where it rested against her neck and the soft, smooth feel of her collar. Memories that made all awareness of his body's pains fade away.

'Hello, sweetheart, you're right on time for supper,' she said, as if he were a husband come home from work and she the doting wife.

The shock of seeing her pristine and alive, dressed in a navy gown that flowed to the floor like silk, was agony. She was beautiful in a way that was otherworldly, that didn't seem possible, and that tore through his insides even more, leaving him feeling like he could only get half a breath—and that was familiar too. He hadn't felt that sensation the first time he had seen her in the wildflower meadow on her family's property.

He had been cutting through, his fishing pole in one hand and a basket in the other for carrying back whatever he hoped to catch. He had not seen her at first: the meadow, like most of the land around Tula, rose and dipped and in some places the wildflowers, a mosaic of pinks, yellows and purples that buzzed with insects, were as tall as him. But he had heard a voice humming a tune.

It was not a spectacular effort, just that of someone who thinks they are alone, and whose mind is wandering. Still, breathing in the sweet, spicy perfume of the flowers, it had made him halt in his march along the trail between them. Of these there were many, as people enjoyed getting lost in the gardens—which the Good Baron, as he was known, enjoyed with a certain level of pride. In the years to come, after he had died, that place had become fenced off, to be enjoyed by a privileged few.

The voice hummed from his left; he remembered trying to spy its owner through the thicket of flowers, knowing somehow that whoever it belonged to was new, that he did not know them as he knew all the people his age. A stranger, his heart had leapt, rejoicing as it always did when the traders came to town.

He followed the sound, his fishing pole and his objective forgotten, the basket banging against his right thigh as he jogged forward. The gardens began to thin on his left, allowing him a glimpse of something white on the other side. Eventually, he came to dip in the land where he was able to see the person humming.

She was alone, dressed in a practical white dress, moving with seemingly no purpose and stopping every few paces to examine a flower or a bee. Her right hand was held out—he remembered that vividly—its palm floating over the tops of the flowers, brushing their tiny petals with her skin.

He knew immediately that he did not know her, and at the very same time he wanted to know everything about her. There was a slight smile, naïve and childish, on her lips as she brushed a hand over the flowers, one that made him feel ashamed for even being able to observe her; the pleasure she was clearly lost in was a private thing.

With his mouth suddenly full of too much salvia, he began to back away, his desire to meet her swallowed by a need to preserve whatever bliss she seemed lost in. Life had other plans, and his heel came down on a dry stick that snapped.

Her voice ceased humming as her head shot up, eyes shadowed by her black fringe. They pinned him where he stood, preventing him from fleeing. He could make out a frown line, one that was stern and unforgiving and that made him think of his mother when she had scolded him as a child.

It was gone in a flash; her lips lifted once more into a smile. Lifting her right hand to shield her eyes from the sun, she asked, 'And who might you be?'

The Carla setting cutlery at the dining table was the same. Gone was the serpentine hiss, and in its place was the light lilt that had been her voice before certain people had ground it down. Alex had never thought he would hear that voice again; the one that she spoke with later in life was a frayed husk of what had been.

'I prepared your favourite,' she said, beaming at him. '*Pelmeni*.'

She stepped back from the head of the table, hands clasped before her. The silk of her dress swayed as she did, its fabric rustling.

Roses as bright as blood flourished upon its bodice. In recognising them—for they were the same as those on the wallpaper of the staircase—Alex felt his agony and awe ignite into anger.

'You're not really her,' he said, tonelessly.

'Of course I'm not; she's dead,' answered Carla with a laugh.

That laugh was confirmation alone that the apparition before him was not Carla, a sharp bark that was all cruelty.

She danced forward, gripped the chair at the head of the table and pulled it out with a creak from its legs. 'But I fooled you for a second.'

She settled herself into the chair, grasping the knife and fork from either side of the plate before her.

'Come take a seat,' she said, pointing with her knife to the chair where a second plate of steaming food sat on her right. Alex refused to move.

'What's out there?' he said, gesturing to the front doors. 'Is it some sort of illusion, a cheap trick to make me feel something? Did I even really leave this place?'

'No, what's outside those doors is completely real,' sighed the Carla-thing while buttering a dumpling with her knife.

Her tone was one of disinterest.

'All of it. I control what exists inside these walls and insides these alone,' speaking with a mouth full of dumpling and minced meat.

'Then how?'

'I could explain to you the mechanics of inter-dimensional travel, but I have a feeling it would go over your provincial head, so I'll dumb it down for you. The world out there is the world you knew in 1840. Beyond these walls is your past—all of it.'

After a pause while Carla sliced into another dumpling Alex wheeled, leaping into a sprint—despite his body's protests—for the twin doors that had remained open all this time. He managed to get several feet before both clapped shut, seemingly of their own power, as the carpet beneath his tired feet unfurled backward and left him running on the spot. This stopped the moment he gave up.

Carla raised her eyebrows from the table.

'See?'

'Then what the hell do you want from me?' screamed Alex.

'Well, I'd like to see that again,' she laughed, mimicking his bug-eyed run from her seat. 'Seriously, though, come have a seat before you keel over.'

'Keel over, what does that even mean?'

The Carla-thing grunted, rolling her eyes. 'I forget sometimes how tiresome it is speaking with time-locked beings. Just relax, I'm not going to hurt you.'

Tentatively, Alex seated himself in a chair three spaces down the table. His aching muscles shrieked with relief.

'You realise the frivolousness of putting distance between us,' she said.

Holding up his hands, palms out, he said, 'I know, just...'

'Okay,' said the Carla-thing, eyes bulging with sarcasm. She continued to eat.

'Is that even real?' he asked.

'It is if I make it real,' she answered, forking another bite into her mouth.

Helplessness drowned him as he sat. He had no idea what to think, so what he asked next he did because it was the most basic of any question: 'What do you want?'

'Now we're getting somewhere. I want to

feed…oh, not like this,' she motioned toward the food, 'this does not satisfy as it would you. I feed on pain, on blood, on the screams of tortured souls. You see, how this usually works is I'll pop up, some stumbling idiot such as yourself comes inside, and I feast.'

'So, you're just… playing with your food?' asked Alex; a feeling of absolute helplessness drained any sort of fear the thing's words inspired.

'That is *exactly* what this is; or it would be, normally,' replied the Carla-thing, dropping her cutlery onto her plate with a clatter.

She wormed her tongue along the flesh behind her upper lip while reaching for a nearby glass of red wine and sipping from it.

'The thing is, I sensed something in you. I've already explained this, but I'll tell you that I get two types of people in here: bumbling idiots and self-righteous pricks; you are neither of those. You, Alexander Nicholai, are filled with wrath for those that intervened in the love you shared for this woman I appear as. Michael, Tomac, Heya, Goodwin… all those conspirators about which it took you *years* to find out, exist beyond the walls of this building, selfishly manipulating the world to benefit them.'

Her words stirred something dark within Alex that had brooded in him for years.

'You remind me of myself,' she said. 'That's why I have spared you, I mean why *have* you, when—if we work together well—I can have so much more to feast on? Plus, the truly wicked always taste better. Thoughts?'

'I'm sorry, what is it you're offering exactly?' he asked, shaking his head in disbelief.

'Revenge, Alex, I'm offering you revenge,' said Carla. Now there was glee and hunger in her voice, eyes bulging wide, lips hooking back into a fiendish grin.

'The death of Luka Ivanov, the Good Baron, has not yet occurred. Carla Ivanov has only just met the wolf in sheep's clothing that is Michael Volkov, but her heart belongs to a young Alex Nicholai, whose own belongs her. You could prevent all that has come to pass, all the pain and turmoil. You could stop it.'

Her words crept up his spine and into his ears with the tickle of spiders' feet, stoking the blaze that existed at his core into a supernova. His eyes beamed with its furious light as he glared at the Carla-apparition, not seeing her but seeing the ancient faces of the people that had ruined his existence on the shores of Lake Silver: old, failing, yet still mocking him with their cruel eyes.

'We just need to bring them here.'

'And how do we do that?' asked Alex, knowing he was damning himself and not caring.

Suddenly the plate before the Carla-thing was capped with a silver cloche.

'Why, we invite them to dinner,' she said, lifting the cloche up.

There, on her plate, was the head of the elder Michael Volkov in a soup of blood.

PART TWO
THE DINNER PARTY

CHAPTER **SIX**

'I can't believe we're doing this,' Tomac Ivanov said over the din of churning wheels and clomping horseshoes as their carriage made its tentative way up the mountain pass carved into the cliff face. Until a week ago, this road had been little more than an uneven cut in the rock that weaved like a worm to nothing.

No longer, it seemed.

'Just saunter up a road that isn't a road, one that kids climb only when they're dared to, for "an evening of great significance,"' he continued, flipping open the invitation letter and reading from it. The page was severely lined in the middle, having been folded and unfolded many times. 'What does that even mean?' he said, and then, without waiting for a reply from to the other passengers, added: 'That Father is *making* us attend is even more of an affront.'

'He's just excited, dear,' said Heya Ivanov, his wife, in a pacifying monotone, staring into her pocket mirror and dabbing at her cheeks.

'He's mad is what he is.'

'He's curious about this stranger—and so are you, may I remind you,' countered Heya in the same disinterested tone.

'I am,' agreed Tomac, his voice growing contemplative and deep. 'Just who exactly is this Viktor Price, and how did he manage to build a house on my land without anyone noticing, land that nobody would think to build on?'

'We would all like an answer to those questions,' said Igor Morozov, opposite the couple. He spoke slowly, his voice so deep that it made Tomac think of coffin lids slamming closed, of cold, silent crypts and death. His occupation, before becoming the head of their family's security and Tula's only semblance of law enforcement, had been that of a soldier. If Tomac were completely honest he would say that the man, with his watchful yet somehow lifeless grey eyes, frightened him. That coupled with the man's unrelenting stiff posture reminded Tomac of a corpse, one slain on a battlefield that, despite its injuries, continued to move by sheer force of will, a will that burned in those icy, lifeless eyes.

Igor had his uses. Everyone did, if you took the time to figure out what they were; something Tomac prided himself on being able to do.

It was unfortunate that his father didn't think so, which was nothing new. Luka Ivanov rarely approved any of his suggestions, much to Tomac's frustration.

Rather than reply to the stoic blond man opposite he nodded and diverted his attention to the window of the carriage. To his right it was fully dark in the valley below; other than the twinkle of lights coming from their vast fortress home, the land was cloaked in gloom. There was still light above in the sky, light of a feeble grey quality that illuminated nothing, making the caps on the mountains appear as jagged black teeth. Nestled in a crook of this darkness farther along the mountain trail were squares of ochre light: their destination.

While the strange, oozing light that spilled from the building's many windows was not enough to reveal its appearance in detail, it did give the impression of its tall, thin spindle-like structure. There was something about it, something that suggested that *it*, and not its mysterious occupant, awaited them with eager excitement.

Tomac did not like it, not one bit. He reclined back in his carriage seat.

'We could be going into a lion's den for all we know,' he muttered.

'Lion's den,' snorted Heya, 'you speak such foolishness sometimes, dear.'

'We know nothing about this Viktor Price.'

Once again Heya snorted, still gazing at her reflection. Tomac ignored her while the word *nothing* tolled like a bell repeatedly in his mind. That was what really flustered him, he realised: the unknowingness of the situation.

He was a firm believer in having a plan and following it; so much so that he knew what the course of his life would be. The invitation letter in his hand did not factor into that plan, arriving less than five days ago at their door, a time frame that was too little for him to gain any knowledge of this Viktor Price, supposedly of Saint Petersburg.

And Michael, the other blow-in, said he

had never heard of him. Except he wasn't a blow-in anymore; now he was a partner.

'I hardly doubt your father would have us walk into anything unsavoury,' said his wife. 'You're wrong,' replied Tomac. 'Unsavoury is exactly the type of thing he would have us wander into. And you're wrong about him being eccentric. He is mad; did you not hear he excused the Fredorovs for being short of their taxes again?'

Heya snapped her pocket mirror closed, her face growing stern as it rounded on her husband in a way that depleted it of all its natural beauty; she looked older, almost crone-like. However, before she could speak, their daughter—who had been quiet to the point that they'd forgotten her—did from beside Igor.

'Grandfather isn't mad, he's just interested in people.'

Carla's voice was assured, the love and admiration for her grandfather clear. Tomac looked at his daughter, who shared his dark hair, but none of his soul, still unable to understand the bizarre creature before him even after eighteen years. She shared her grandfather's kind-heartedness, yet none of the jovial idiocy that led him to do silly, embarrassing things like joining the peasants in their drinking hole with a blatant disregard for social decorum. She was a dreamer instead.

'I think this is a discussion for another time,' said Heya curtly, giving him a look that he agreed with. It was foolish to talk so openly about such things, even around his daughter who, to him, lived in a fairy-tale. While this was true, if Tomac had known exactly what his daughter was dreaming of that led her to be so forgettable and quiet he might have grown concerned. Not because her dreams were actually memories of earlier today, by the brook with the farm boy who sometimes cleaned out their stables, but because those memories were not rose-tinted, or naïve; instead, there was a practicality about them.

There was lust too, and not just for the boy but for what the boy represented, what they talked about in their secret rendezvous, months' worth at this point. Freedom, freedom from rules, from the life their parents had told them they had to live.

Tomac would have grown concerned indeed.

'Don't worry, sir. Nothing will befall your

family while I remain at your side,' assured Igor in his entombing tones.

'Thank you, Igor. That is a comfort, and I think we are here,' said Heya.

Carla Ivanov stepped down from the carriage, happy to have some distance between herself and Igor's aftershave. It was rich and musky and he smelt like he bathed in it, or at least furiously scrubbed his skin with it. This made her smile as she could not imagine her father's bodyguard undressed for some reason; if someone had told her that he slept in the pristine suits he wore, she would have believed them.

'Do you find something amusing?' asked her mother, whose voice suggested that nothing of the sort ought to be found right now.

Glancing around as the other carriages formed a semi-circle in the light cast by the insidious house, Carla agreed with her. It's like it's watching me, she thought. Its windows were like eyes, yellow eyes that were sick, poisoned and hungry.

'Carla?' Her mother again, and hearing that clipped, frightened chirp in her voice was like a blow to the head. Carla had never heard fright in her mother's voice before. Suddenly her heart was hammering in her chest, thumping to get out.

'It's nothing,' she replied, breathless.

As Heya Ivanov nodded at her, all those invited, a collection of Tula's high society, gathered before the stone steps of the house. Its double doors, engrained with images of wildflowers, flung open. A man stepped out, dressed all in black as if attending a funeral, his hair and beard silver in a style she had never seen before. The word it conjured in her mind was *trim*.

'Good evening my neighbours,' he said, with a smile that put a pang of recognition in her mind. 'It's wonderful to see you all.'

'Is it?' replied her father, glancing around the gloomy precipice of the courtyard, his tone disapproving in a way that Carla knew well; despite this, her shoulders still tensed on hearing it. Her father had a talent for putting his worst foot forward when it came to social situations. Something her mother recognised as well, judging by the slow eye roll she performed. Carla didn't have to be a mind reader to hear her thoughts: not again, they sighed, causing the smirk to return to her face.

Sometimes she found her parents to be funny in a way that was childish and unknown to them.

'Hush now,' said Luka Ivanov in a quiet voice. His gaze was gentle, amused on the surface yet cautioning underneath to her father, who looked away like a sullen child put in his place. For now. That gaze swept round, brightening as it did until her grandfather was observing the greeting gentleman.

'I apologise,' he said graciously, 'what I think my son meant to say was that this location is a strange place to consider "wonderful". Wouldn't you say so?'

Carla's smirk widened into a grin; she knew her grandfather long enough to know what he was doing, that while his words could be considered offensive, they were spoken in the guise of a curious inquisition. She had never seen anyone flustered by his light conversational tone, whereas everything her father said sounded like an accusation. It was a skill she hoped to master one day.

The stranger on the steps above looked down at them sheepishly, his shoulders drawing high and close, lips smiling tightly while his eyes lit with awkward embarrassment. She knew that look, the pang of recognition striking her so hard this time that it was like a fist to her abdomen, expelling the air from her lungs.

'What is it now?' hissed her mother in a venomous whisper.

Carla didn't reply; instead, she watched with wide eyes as the stranger descended the steps, thinking: This is not good, this is not good at all.

'I believe it is I who must apologise,' he said. 'I have a rather unorthodox enjoyment of the more morbid things in life; it is why I have come to build my home in such a peculiar place. Viktor Price, at your service.'

The stranger who, despite his age, moved with a surprising swiftness, had reached her grandfather, offering his hand to shake. Luka Ivanov accepted it without pause, and she couldn't help but note the similarities between the two even though they looked nothing alike; their height might have been the same, if her grandfather's shoulders hadn't started to stoop over. The stranger's trim hair and beard showed a face that was youthful despite his obvious age, while her grandfather's long mane of soot-grey hair could not hide a fragility that had entered him in recent years, one that had come with age and tugged at her heart whenever she saw it.

Even with these differences Carla saw a shared community in the two men, a kindness and affection that glinted in their eyes and hugged their smiles. They did not look like strangers as they shook hands, but friends that had not seen each other for some time. It warmed the tender spot in her heart she held for Luka Ivanov, to see that fragility be cast away, forgotten by the warmth of this stranger. That was enough to calm the reservations forming in her toward Mr. Price.

It was one of the last moments she would ever remember seeing kindness in Price's face.

'Carla, what is wrong with you?' asked her mother as her grandfather exchanged pleasantries.

'Nothing, Mama… nothing,' she murmured.

Heya Ivanov frowned at her daughter, wondering if she needed to remain with the carriages and horses that she loved so much. She moved, meaning to pinch the soft flesh of Carla's upper arm to whisper warnings in her ear; a thing she often did whenever her daughter troubled her, when the stranger spoke to them all.

'But there is a wonderfulness in this grey place,' announced Viktor Price. He gestured to the very edge of the precipice, where through the dead skeletal limbs of a white tree the lights of Tula flickered in the dark of the valley below. 'Wouldn't you say that is a wonderful sight?'

Luka Ivanov lurched through the turning group, using his wolf-headed cane to follow Price to the edge. Wind gusted, ruffling the sooty strands of his fringe and rippling the scarlet cloth of his coat that flowed behind him. In that moment Carla saw him as the young man he used to be, when he went into the world, leaving Tula to explore, something her own father had declined doing.

'Yes, I believe it is,' he said.

A chorus of agreement rose from the crowd. Carla spotted Father Goodwin amongst its members, his eyes bleary, his beard unkempt and moist-looking. Even her mother was distracted by the view, linking her fingers with her husband's.

She became aware of a presence at her side.

'Think he's going to push the old man off the edge?' asked Michael Volkov.

The tall boy—she could never think of him as a man—laughed, his lips pulling back to show pink gums as well as teeth. Teeth that were far too white to be real, a sight that was more comical than unappealing.

Carla laughed, a hearty bark that caused Michael's grin to grow even more, unaware that she was laughing at his ridiculously porcelain teeth rather than his joke.

Thunder crackled in the grey clouds swarming over the mountain peaks behind the house. Being this high, however, meant that their voluminous noise happened all around them, causing several of their troop to gasp and Brania Maca, the coin collector's wife, to shriek. Those around her, including her husband Kazimir, giggled as she smiled, hand on her chest.

While the others chuckled nervously amongst themselves, Carla spotted the tall, shadowed figure standing in the open doorway of the house. They were haloed in that ochre glow that stretched out onto the stone; still her eyes could not pierce the shadow that cloaked them. Nor did they move from their bizarre stance, arms held out from their sides, crooked at the elbow as if to make themselves appear as wide as possible, when she noticed them.

Surely she sees me, thought Carla, not knowing why she'd automatically considered this person to be female.

The feeling of being watched returned, only a hundred times more intense. This time it did not radiate from the windows of the house but from the dark shape in the doorway and Carla found that all interest in her surroundings had fallen away; even the insidious house itself no longer matter to her. All that did was escaping that feeling, which seemed to root her in place on the stone plateau, turning her flesh into a squirming thing that wrestled to part from her bones.

Nauseating thoughts scuttled over her mind, telling her that it wasn't the shape of a person, it was a void, a window into another realm without light, or time. A place that, were you to sink into it, would be like falling through honey forever.

'I think that's a sign we should be getting inside,' announced Price.

His prompt, cheerful tone snapped through the miasma that had imprisoned her, setting her free. Carla felt her body unlock, the sickening thoughts dissipating into whatever nothingness they had come from. She wanted to laugh, only she knew that if she did it would come out as a sob. And the shadow in the doorway was gone.

In its place was the figure of a thin spindle of a man standing like a soldier at attention. She overheard Price say, 'I'll have my man, Solomon, take care of your coachmen,' and assumed this was the thin man he was referring to.

He led them up the house steps, their crowd funnelling into two lines to climb, wind whooping at their heels. Carla followed reluctantly at the rear, wringing her hands as warning signs flashed in her head.

You should not go in, you should not go in, they flashed in deep red.

'Solomon Hil, at your service' said the gaunt butler, darting forward to shake her grandfather's hand. Even from the bottom step, Carla could see that he was so tall he had to bend to do so, light gleaming off of his bald pate. His lips were hooked in a grin that looked all mischief to her, making the skin of her back vibrate the way a tuning fork does, making her want to cringe and even scream.

He was dressed like their host, all in black except for a stiff white shirt beneath his waistcoat and tails. A small scribble of a moustache, also black, crowned his lip like a furry caterpillar. Both it and his clothes were creaseless, as if they were made of ink or oil, as if they weren't real.

No one seemed to notice this as the queue shuffled forward until she was the only one left.

'And this is my granddaughter, Carla,' Luka said, introducing her to Price.

The butler had retreated inside the house, taking their coats, engaging them in conversation. Already, he had Goodwin belly-laughing.

Carla turned to their host as he took her offered hand between fingers that were calloused, but gentle, and found herself looking into the eyes of Alexander Nicholai.

CHAPTER **SEVEN**

1

Carla Ivanov could hear the crackle of the fireplace as she and the other guests sipped vodka in the study of the house, its bookshelf walls choked with leather-bound tomes, its rectangular space furnished with regal furniture in reds and golds. She heard everything as if it were from a distant room. The polite titter of laughter as Price told jokes, emitting charm as he stood beside the mighty mantlepiece. Even the soft velvet of the sofa cushions at her back were far away to her.

She was travelling in time, leaving her body behind, the noise of fire gnawing on wood transforming in her ears, becoming water flowing in a stream. The noxious musk of Igor Morozov's aftershave faded, replaced by the scent of sun-soaked grass and the calming aroma of basil. The same thing occurred with the conversation as her mind stretched back down a long corridor to earlier that day, turning into the sound of stones being skipped over the surface of water.

The skipper, who had just loosed another smooth stone across the brackish river, caught her gaze over his shoulder, his right arm still extended from his throw.

'What?' Alexander Nicholai grinned, his lips splitting into a smile that contained embarrassment and joy.

Carla shook her head, causing the waves of her black hair to sway. 'Nothing.'

'Are you daydreaming again? What about?' asked the young man who was her friend and so much more.

When she replied it was not her memory she was witnessing: she was there, having somehow travelled back in time to the green banks of the river. She sat in the shade of trees, which meant she didn't have to squint to see him.

'The same things I always seem to be dreaming about lately,' she answered, smiling.

She smiled differently around him. There was no overthinking with him, no second-guessing, or gameplay. With him her walls could come down; she loved that vulnerable feeling, and feared it, feared what it meant.

'Of leaving, of running away to somewhere new. Childish fantasises.'

'Are they really?' He skipped his last stone. It bobbled over the water's black surface, creating three circular ripples before sinking. Then he joined her on the grass, his body humming with the heat of the sun, smelling of work and dirt.

'Unfortunately, yes,' she said, linking her arm with his, resting her cheek against it.

'They don't have to be.' His tone was delightful, frivolous of the conventions that held them both. 'If we do what we want, if we don't let them decide our fate for us, those dreams can be a reality.'

She smiled at him, looking into his glacier eyes. Although it was a smile that did not run through her completely: in her heart it met a link, a chain link that tugged with quiet pain.

'Where are you?' asked a voice.

It belonged to Michael Volkov, who wore an expression she found she didn't like. It was cruel in the way a child can look when they have something no one else has and they choose to lord it over their peers. Michael looked like that, his fake teeth showing through his parted lips.

Carla blinked at him, hoping that he was the only one that had noticed her dreaming. 'Daydreaming,' she smiled at him, though it felt pasted on.

If Michael noticed, he didn't seem to show it, shaking his head. 'You women, always with your head in the clouds,' he commented, then he added, 'are you going to finish that?'

He was pointing at the glass of vodka she had been given; it sat untouched on the small mahogany table against the sofa's armrest. She handed it to him without a word, her eyes on the butler who stood once more in the threshold of the study, hands clasped behind his back. His face wasn't quite like a skull; more like a skull that had a thin veneer of waxy skin stretched over it.

He was smirking at them all as Price, whose eyes were those of the young man that she held in her heart, engaged the cream of Tula's high society, asking questions about the land, the people and not providing much in the way of answers other than explaining for a good fifteen minutes about how the lights were powered by something called "electricity". Apparently, it was all the craze in Saint Petersburg; faces gawked at him and her grandfather praised mankind's ingenuity.

As if registering her gaze upon him, Solomon Hil raised his voice. 'Dinner is ready, sir,' he announced, 'if your guests would like to follow me across the hall to the dining area.'

He gestured with a swish of his left arm to the room behind him.

'About time, I am starving,' proclaimed Father Goodwin in jest.

Several of their group laughed heartedly,

though from their strained expressions Carla could discern that the laughter was false. She instantly felt sorry for the father, who, from how he laughed along, she guessed was unaware of how the others viewed him, knowing from overheard conversations that it was his gluttonous drinking that disgusted them. While his behaviour was sometimes uncouth, she saw that beneath that jesting exterior and ruddy, grinning face was something not far from the crying children she had seen parting from their mothers on the first day of school.

'Excellent,' said Price, gesturing to Solomon, 'if you'd all like to follow my man.'

People rose from their seats, glasses in hand. She caught Price glancing at her: little more than a flicker of his gaze, then it returned to the carpeted floor until he passed her.

Before, she had believed it was simply her father's paranoia that had caused him to be suspicious of Price, the same way he was with anything new. Now she knew different, she knew there was something wrong here; and yet, other than her father, who had sat quietly sulking as their host put on his show, she seemed to be the only one aware of how strange this all was.

They were inside a house that had not existed a week ago.

That was what they had all been saying after receiving their invitations, disbelieving that a building like this could simply be constructed in secret, and now it was… forgotten. All that indignity, that bizarre, hurt sense of pride as if Price had pulled the wool over their eyes, was gone.

Carla couldn't understand it and intended to find out more.

'If we are dining now, would it be too much trouble if I used the facilities before sitting down?' asked Kazimir Maca.

'But of course you can,' said Solomon Hil, bending in the middle somewhat as he spoke as if going to bow.

His smile, Carla found, was like a sneer.

'Why, isn't this all lovely,' cooed Brania Maca, scanning the dining table as her husband drifted down a dimly lit corridor per the butler's instruction. 'Such fine designs, and these plates! Aren't they beautiful?'

'Yes, they are,' agreed Heya as she took a chair opposite, her back to the crackling fireplace.

Carla paid no thought to the smirk that fluttered across her mother's face, or how something in Brania's face seemed to pinch, shutting off her awed emotion; she was distracted by the table's finery. Her plate, which was enamel-white and hot to touch, was detailed with a nettle of black vines that ended in roses, their red colour more vividly bright than any shade she'd ever seen. The metal of her knife and fork were engraved to look like wildflowers, as too was the silver goblet before her.

'Indeed,' seconded her grandfather, taking the seat left of the head of the table.

'Only the finest for tonight's company,' said Price.

He looked out of place at the table's head, uncomfortable, his expression sheepish in its smile while his eyes never settled on any of their gazes. Without a word, a line of maids dressed in black and white marched out from a recess behind Price to encircle the table, filling goblets and serving food within seconds before vanishing back through what Carla only assumed was a door leading to the kitchen.

'And some effort, I must imagine,' said Tomac, raising his goblet. 'Getting all this stuff, all these staff here without anyone noticing, must have taken some work.'

'It did,' said Price.

His voice was cold. His wandering gaze now held her father's the way a trap holds a paw. Her father appeared not to notice, his countenance one of mild interest as he stirred the wine in his goblet by rotating his wrist. The tick-tock of the antique grandfather clock became deafening from the hall as their silence drew out.

'Well, I'm sure that the Empire would greatly appreciate those stealthy skills in their ongoing efforts in Caucasus.'

A murmur of faux laughter rumbled from the seated table, the loudest coming from Goodwin, who had already drained his drink. The only one that seemed outside the laughter was Brania who, frowning petulantly, glancing between the plates of steaming food on the table to the hallway behind her.

'Kazimir is going to miss this,' she whined, clearly unaware of the tension that hung thick over the table.

'I'm sure he'll be back shortly,' said Heya in a voice like honey, 'and if not I'll happily feed it to you.'

Brania blushed, her hands nervously rising to pat her glossy dark curls while Carla's mother continued to grin across from her, fork and knife clasped in her hands. Both women began to eat daintily, unperturbed by the others' lack of reaction.

Only Carla seemed to notice it.

Father Goodwin had commenced eating with aplomb, mouth slapping with the food shovelled inside, producing low-pitched grunts of satisfaction as he chewed. The rest did not move but watched the exchange between the head and bottom of the table taking place in its silences as much as in what was spoken.

'That's funny,' said Price finally. He reclined back in his chair, sipping wine as if settling down before a fire after a long day's work, not a formal dinner, his long legs thrust out beneath the table. 'And I suppose that's something of a compliment coming from yourself, Tomac.'

Being addressed in a way that suggested Price knew him made her father's forehead crease. It was the first sign of a crack in the armour she had seen him wear inside the house. One made of cold, detached and malicious indifference as if nothing of his host was interesting or worth engaging with; she had seen him use it countless times to conceal the ferocious paranoia and jealousy that writhed within him. Carla hated it, the part of him that had led the conversation in the carriage ride up the mountain. It was somehow weak and pitiful as well as something to be feared, and worse than that she did not see her father when he was this way.

She saw something close to a monster.

'What do you mean by that?' asked Tomac, keeping his composure.

'Yes, what do you mean?' remarked Luka Ivanov, his grey brow knitted together in confusion.

Having the same question asked by her grandfather seemed to break Price's smug resolve. Like rock that had been smashed aside to reveal a thread of gold, Carla saw genuine care in his silver bearded face towards the aged Baron.

'I'm sorry it has come to this, but there was no other way,' he said to Luka, then turned to address her father.

What Carla had previously thought was smugness was back, only now she could see that it was hate, hate that steeled the light in his eyes and drew the skin around them tight. He faced her father from the head of the table like a knight ready for battle.

'What I mean is that when Tomac Ivanov compliments you on acting stealthy it is high praise indeed, seeing as it comes from the master of the sly and secretive.'

'This is lovely, isn't it,' cooed Brania across the table.

'Most fine,' echoed Goodwin, his plump

face as red as a freshly picked apple.

'It is; I especially love the *Pelmeni*,' said Heya.

'Thank you, I'll pass your compliments on to the chef.' This was Solomon Hil, bowing in the middle once more by the entrance where he stood as if on guard. His lips pulled back as if on invisible hooks, revealing yellowed teeth. It made the wizened, stretched skin of his head look even closer to ripping apart and showing the skull underneath. Bizarrely, only she noticed this.

None of the other diners turned to the sound of his voice. His words hummed with glee.

'You know what would make this even more fun,' said Heya, with a type of jubilation in her voice that Carla had never heard before.

'What?' asked Brania.

With that, her mother scraped her chair backward, threw down her napkin, marched round the table and collapsed into the seat beside Brania, the one her husband should have been occupying. Briefly, a thought fluttered across Carla's mind—what was taking Kazimir so long?—then her mother started to feed the coin collector's wife from the woman's own plate.

Brania hummed as her lips clamped over the food on Heya's fork. She licked her bottom lip, her tongue catching a runaway morsel of dumpling.

'Oh, it looks like it's trying to escape,' laughed Heya, and it was this laugh that seemed to Carla to be all the more shocking than anything else.

She had never heard her mother sound so carefree.

Again, everyone at the table seemed blind to the sudden display of affection between the two women. Carla tried to remember ever having seen either of them act this way before and couldn't. Yet, their behaviour seemed to indicate that it wasn't new. Everyone else bar Goodwin, who was continuing to guzzle down food, ignored this, transfixed by the two men on either side of the long table.

'I'm sure I don't know what you are referring to, sir,' replied her father, mustering an incredulous, disgusted tone. 'Nor do I much like your thinly-veiled attempt to disgrace my reputation in front of my family, or members of my community. How dare you, stranger, insult me at this event that you've clearly organised to do only that?'

The man who claimed himself to be Viktor Price chuckled in his seat. It made Carla's already frightened heart squeeze with fear.

Oh no, she thought, please, no, knowing from Price's bitter laugh that her father had in some way wounded their host in the past.

'I forgot how much of a pretentious *prick* you used to be. I suppose in my time you've gotten all you wanted, so there's no longer any point in pretending.'

'Insanity,' spat Tomac, 'we are in the presence of insanity.'

'Let the mask fall down, Ivanov. Show your real face—the face of a man that would kill his own father just get his title sooner,' replied Price with a relaxed venom.

CHAPTER **EIGHT**

1

'We need to leave,' Carla squeaked.

Her voice felt like an ancient, dried-up hinge draped in cobwebs; it was no surprise no one had heard her. Or maybe they just couldn't, the same way no one but her seemed to see her mother feeding Brania like a lover lost in some sort of romantic pageantry, or Father Goodwin—having finished with the food on his plate—reaching out to seize the plates of others. Carla watched him stand, lean across the table, and snatch the plate in front of Michael Volkov before collapsing back into his chair. Michael's eyes flicked to Goodwin as he began to ingest, fork posed in his right hand, unperturbed.

'We need to leave,' she squeaked again.

Louder this time, a hitch in her voice.

Terror caused it, catching her diaphragm, causing it to flounder uselessly as it rose like a clot in her veins. She could feel it slowly travelling along the highway of her bloodstream like a rock in her blood as it crested over her collar to the base of her neck.

Her heart was a thunderstorm in her chest.

Carla looked to her father for help, who seemed to be like a fish out of water, his lips opening and closing as his slate eyes glared at Price.

'What is this? What are you talking about?' questioned her grandfather, his furry eyebrows knitted together in a single grey line.

'Go on, tell him, Tomac,' said Price softly, amused yet righteous. 'Tell him what you and your dear wife have been scheming behind your chamber doors. How you plan on enlisting the help of Michael Volkov in killing your father by offering your daughter's hand in marriage. How you plan to take over the Barony of Tula because you feel your old man has grown soft, how you plan on raising the land tax because it pains you to think that the common people see Luka Ivanov as a bleeding heart to take advantage of. Go on, tell him.'

Whatever her father meant to say next was interrupted by Brania Maca.

'Where is that man?' she sighed, angry now. 'He's missing everything.'

'You know what,' said Heya, 'let's go looking for him.'

She offered her left hand, palm up. Brania looked at it for a second, smiled and slapped her right on top of it.

In a flurry of dress skirts, both women ran out of the room into the hallway like children at play. Carla could hear their laughter, also child-like, diminishing in volume as they disappeared to the left. For some reason this seemed to cause her father to launch back in his chair, legs scraping, and stand.

'Where do you think you're going?' he yelled.

This caused Igor, who occupied the seat to her father's right, to mimic his stance, only his dead eyes no longer looked so disinterested. They blazed in his corpse-like face and Carla realised that he was enjoying this; she could feel his itch to lash out, to cause some act of violence. It pulsated from him and in her mind, she saw a swarm of flies withering over the bloated body of a slaughtered cow on some distant battlefield. She knew that was what he saw in his head in such tense moments, and that the only way to silence it was to feel skin rip underneath his fingernails.

Carla paled, staring at Igor while seeing a window into his mind. Her body was chilled by what she saw, the skin of her arms erupting with goose flesh. 'Dad,' she yelled, finding her voice. 'We need to leave, now.'

And it worked. Whatever enchantment lay over them seemed to be expelled.

Tomac Ivanov looked at her with his slate eyes and frowned, gripping the table as his legs seemed to fold. To her left, she heard Goodwin cease scratching cutlery over ceramic. Even the fireplace seemed to quieten at her command, leaving the only noise that of the ceaseless ticking clock. And in that almost-silence, Carla breathed in the scent of the table: the food, which had appeared so wholesome, reeked of rot. To her horror she saw that nothing more than black mould lay on their plates, abuzz with flies. No one else seemed to notice but her.

'You can leave,' a voice said to her.

Carla's head turned on bones that felt

arthritic and pained until she was staring at Price. He looked at her with a concern she couldn't fathom and once more thought of her young lover. 'It's been agreed that you can leave, and it would be wise if you did.'

'Yes, we'll leave,' Tomac said, his voice strained. He shook his head; the others at the table were doing the same. 'But not before we've found your mother.'

Tomac launched toward the hallway and Carla followed, hearing chair legs shriek across wooden boards behind her. She was several feet behind him, having to dart around the table, which stank of overly sweet, moist rot, hitching up the navy skirt of her dress to do so. Tomac shouted Heya's name upon spying her, charging across a vast hexagonal room that housed a grand staircase. In the distance, Carla saw the backs her mother's and Brania's bodies vanish into the darkness of an opening on the room's other side. Her father was halfway across this space when the opening slammed shut with an echoing *boom*.

The sound resonated throughout the house, vibrating the very air, filling Carla's heart with ice and halting her pursuit on the room's threshold. Her father had stopped too, right in the centre.

The hexagon did not have doors. Its entrances, which sat at all four points of the compass, were simply arched openings. Staring across the vast, carpeted space, she saw that it wasn't a door that had clapped shut, prohibiting their chase; it was a wall, decorated in the same forest motif as the rest of the room: a dark navy background snaked through with silver vines flowering into roses at their ends.

It was as if the opening that her mother had exited through had not existed at all.

'You asked a lot questions about this house, Mister Ivanov,' said Solomon Hil, his voice echoing throughout the vast chamber.

His teasing tone was clear.

'You never asked the most important one: is it *safe*?' he said, raising his right eyebrow.

2

The entrances to the east and west shut with mighty booms, one after the other, causing Tomac's head to snap in each direction. Again, there was no sign of any door being closed on a hinge, more a sense of movement out of the corner of the eye, and walls filled the space where chances of escape had been. Carla's father was hyperventilating now, his skin pale, his eyes wide and darting as panic set in.

'Can one of you fools stop gawking and help me,' Tomac commanded.

No one moved over the threshold, all of them understanding that it was not a room anymore but a killing floor. It was a death trap, reminding Carla of a meadow a hunter would position themselves downwind of, hiding in the undergrowth and waiting for whatever beast they had tracked to enter.

And her father stood in its centre.

She moved without thought, meaning to dart for him, believing that if she could somehow reach him, she could save him. A hand, strong and unyielding, seized upon her left forearm, spinning her into arms that were like prison bars.

They belonged to none other than Viktor Price.

'No,' she cried, trying to fight while unable to take her eyes from the scene. 'I need to save him.'

'Would he do the same for you?' Price shouted at her. 'Would he?'

His gruff voice sliced through the hysteria that consumed her, sapping at the strength with which she fought him. Carla stared up into his iceberg-blue eyes, saw neither hate nor rage; instead, there was a pleading sense of finality.

His words echoed within her head, trying to tell her something her mind was too distraught to catch. Arms encircled her waist from behind, pulling her from Price's grip: they were Michael Volkov's. She observed disgust flicker across Price's expression as she was tugged away by the young blond man, then he was adjusting his suit jacket, stepping forward to address her father.

'I used to be so frightened of you,' he said.

'I don't even know who you are,' screamed Tomac. He seemed unable to move, his legs trembling beneath by his fear. Sweat lashed his pale brow.

'No, but I imagine that's quite common with most of the people you fuck over. They are shadows to you in the wake of your path. I was a boy then, raised to be fearful and respectful of those above me because they are better, somehow. It's only through life that I've learned what a crock of shit that is: you are no better than I, just another bug crawling in the dirt for what little power they can hope to gain.'

'You're mad, all of this is just madness,' Tomac screamed, legs jittering, tears streaming.

Luka Ivanov grasped at Price's collar with feeble fingers. 'Whatever this is, please stop,' he said. 'That's my child in there. I know there is cruelty in him, but please have mercy.'

Price looked at Luka, disappointment breaking through his stony façade. 'I'm sorry, I'm not the one in charge.'

All eyes turned to Solomon Hil. He stood, hands clasped behind his back, his spindle-like appearance agonising to look at, shoulders hunched as if his gaunt body couldn't properly hold them up in a suit as black as tar. It even seemed to shine like the surface of the thick, vicious liquid when the soft lamplight hit it.

'Tomac Ivanov, you have been judged by a courtroom of your peers and deemed guilty, not only of the things you have done, but the things you are going to do, and as such you will bleed for those sins. We bleed in this house, son.'

No one else but Tomac saw the eyes of the butler fill with blood, the whites becoming red until the man, still grinning his sickle-like grin, had rubies for eyes.

'Igor, won't you save him?' shrieked Carla.

This seemed to break the fear that had frozen her father's bodyguard. He began fumbling at the hatchet, a souvenir from his time as a soldier, that he kept concealed beneath his jacket. Carla had seen him sharpening the blade, an ornate piece of metal decorated with various lines to look like crashing waves.

When she wheeled back, she saw that the

roses, the ones sewn into the thread of the hexagonal room's walls, were glowing, the red in them blooming until they blazed brighter than lantern light, than firelight, and her father staggered below them, his head shifting all around as if trying to take it all in at once. Watching them grow brighter and brighter until they seemed to bulge out of the dark walls, Carla felt a pressure in the air building, mounting to a breaking point.

One of the roses exploded. Then another and another. They erupted into fountains of blood, thick and dark, that gushed into the chamber below, splashing onto the carpet until the entire space begun to flood. A tide of red poured at them, forcing them to backpedal until it struck the threshold of the room, where it splashed back as if there was glass there so clean it was unnoticeable.

Already the tide was up to her father's knees, causing him to wade as he tried to reach them. His eyes were wide, white orbs in his head, bulging with fright. They made him look child-like to Carla, for she had never seen such hysteria before. It seemed to have stripped him of all his pompous, spoilt bravado, reducing him to a child once more.

Cascades of blood rained down in thick

streams, raising the red sludge at his knees to waist height in seconds. Splatters of it coated him. Eventually, a freshly spouting stream stuck him, ploughing him underneath the blood pool.

The air stank of copper.

'Daddy,' she screamed, collapsing to her knees in Michael's arms. Tears burned from her weeping eyes.

The opening which they stared through was a bloody wall now. She could no longer hear the sounds of rushing liquid.

'I believe it was the butler in the pantry,' said Solomon Hil, amused.

A second later, Igor swung the blade of his hatchet into the back of Solomon's skull.

PART THREE
HOUSE RULES

CHAPTER **NINE**

The *crack* of Igor's hatchet burying itself in Solomon Hil's skull reminded Carla of a cord of wood, too dense for the blade, becoming stuck. All breathing had stopped in that dimly-light place where a passageway had once stood; in its place was a navy wall of thread, snaked through with silver vines. There were figures in those vines, hunters and animals, all staring as Hil staggered forward on the carpeted floor. Choking sounds emitted from his throat as a glob of blood spilled out over his lips onto his chin. Streams of it ran from each nostril.

Even Carla's heart felt like it had stopped, waiting for this nightmare to be over, for the man that had by some witchcraft drowned her father in a cauldron of blood. It seemed that the others were of the same mind because all eyes were on him.

Igor had stepped back, letting go of the hatchet's handle as blood blossoms bloomed around the cleft driven into the curve of Hil's skull. It trickled down the base of the gaunt man's neck, soaking into the black collar of his fine jacket.

The wet choking sounds clicking from his throat transformed into laughter. Full-blown, eye-watering belly laughs.

'That was delicious,' announced Hil, with the hatchet still buried in his head.

He didn't wheel round to them; instead, his bones began to snap like dry kindling inside the meat of his body. His clothes shuddered and rippled like a black sack full of hungry rats swarming to get out. The place where his shoulders should be was hitching up and down, causing his arms to flop about in a frenzy of movement.

Carla heard Michael's gasp, his hands losing their grip on her arms as he backed away. The others were doing the same, backstepping as this spindle-like figure, his legs planted together to make him look even stranger, writhed. She could see the bones of his skull separating; they bulged against the taut skin of his head, threatening to rip it open as they rearranged beneath his flesh.

Igor's hatchet dropped from the wound and into Hil's palms. An impossible thing, as a person's forearms can't bend that far at the elbows; but they had done so. It was then, staring into what had been the back of Hil's head, that Carla understood what was happening. He was turning around to face them; he was *rearranging* himself to.

Just as she thought it, a pair of iris-black eyes opened, a stump of a nose punched itself out, and a smile split the skin where Igor's axe had buried itself. It was red-rimmed on account of the blood, making Hil look like a greedy child that had been eating jam.

'Run,' Carla screamed, grabbing a fistful of her dress and fleeing.

2

Alex watched as Carla, Michael and Luka dashed into the corridor on the right. Igor, startled by the lady's shriek, darted off into the opposite corridor, his jacket fanning behind him like wings. Goodwin did not flee; instead he grasped the crucifix that hung on a beaded chain from around his neck and raised it.

The apparition that the house was guised as jerked its head at him.

'See,' it said, its voice a serpentine rasp. 'I told you about these people.'

'Remember what we discussed, Carla doesn't come to harm,' Alex said, dashing after the trio who had already disappeared round a corner.

'Yes, yes, of course,' he heard the creature answer, and then it said to Goodwin, 'That, unfortunately, does not apply to you.'

The House pointed the hatchet at Goodwin, his ruddy jowls quivering as he fought to regain some sense of composure, his crucifix held out from his body. The House took a step toward him, weighing up the hatchet in both hands. Off to the left, the grandfather clock continued to swing, only its pace was swifter, its golden pendulum whipping back and forth at a blur.

'Stay away from me, demon!' Goodwin blurted out.

The House inhaled deeply from the blood-rich air, its faux eyelids closing to draw strength.

'I am a man of faith; you cannot harm me.'

'Funny, you don't smell of faith, you smell of fear—and not the fun kind,' answered the House.

It marched forward in its current guise, its long, thin legs covering the distance before Goodwin's dizzied mind had time to react, its stride sure. He watched as the thing reared back its right arm, the one holding the hatchet, bringing the blade over its shoulder and down through Goodwin's outstretched right hand.

Pain lit up like a bright lance inside his

head as he gasped, dropping his black crucifix to the carpet. Goodwin gripped at his hand only for his fingers to instantly become drenched in the blood spewing from the wound; there was now a gap of raw, bleeding flesh between his index finger and the one beside it.

Staggering backward, he looked toward the creature just as it brought the hatchet down again. This time the blade slashed across his left collar bone, no more than a superficial injury on account of his thick clothes, yet the force of the swing was enough to bring him to his knees. In the time it had taken him to assess this the creature had rounded up his arm; Goodwin saw the thing's mashed teeth, all yellowed and crooked, gritted together in fiendish delight, its stretched cheeks spotted with his blood as the hatchet cleaved into his forehead.

Warm, liquid rained over his face, painting the world in crimson. There was a sense of movement, of speed beyond the scarlet lens and then pain, boundless and sharp, so sharp it became everything Goodwin knew. Then there was nothing.

CHAPTER **TEN**

1

Igor skidded around the hallway corner, his breathing a sharp, hitching rasp through dry lips, only to halt at what lay before him. The new corridor was different, brighter; there were still silver branches in the threaded walls, only the background had changed to the pale blue of an October sky. But that wasn't what shocked all sense of flight from his legs: it was the bodies.

They lay strewn about the hall in heaps and piles, all coated in the same dust grey that Igor knew to be muck. He knew the fields that muck had come from, churned up by horse hooves and charging men, their spilt blood mixing it into a thick paste that suffocated your pores. Igor had seen men drown in that grey paste, screaming as either the weight of dead men or horses sunk them further into the ooze until they were choking on it.

'Oh no,' he whispered, his eyes staring like great lamps filled with fright.

Sweat left trails down his corpse-stiff face as dread became a lump of steel in his stomach. Even with that grey coating he recognised the uniform, remembered the itchiness of it against his shoulders.

'Oh no, no, no, no.'

He could smell the putrid stink of decay, of fly-bloated flesh ready to rupture with rot and turned gaseous, all beneath the cloying scent of grey muck, and knew he would not venture there. Igor turned to leave, sweat like ice on him, and saw the corridor that he had come from elongate before his eyes. The more he walked towards it the further it lengthened, the further the corner stretched away from him like some surreal mirage. His walk became a trot that became a jog that became a run. Still, the corner he had dashed around waned into insignificance.

Igor ceased sprinting with a whimper, bowing over in the middle, gasping for air, his lungs on fire. When he raised his head the sight remained unchanged: both blue walls stretched out seamlessly on either side of him beyond his vision, maybe to infinity.

'What's going on?' he whined, tears raining down on his high cheeks.

Igor knew what he would find on turning back. Had that body moved?

He squinted at the first body; it lay on its front in a diagonal line across the hall, its face turned away so all he saw was mud-clumped hair. He could have sworn its left arm had been underneath its cheek, not lying palm-down on the carpet.

Igor inhaled, foul air slicing across his teeth.

He knew what he had to do to get out of this nightmare, but the thought of nearing one of those corpses rooted his feet to the spot. Eventually, he managed to raise his left foot and step forward, dread growing even heavier in his stomach while his bladder felt pinched to screaming point. There was no sound but the in/out of air over his teeth and the depression each of his approaching footfalls made in the thick carpeted floor.

Moving slow, arms out, fingers splayed as if to catch something, he became aware of just how much his feet sunk into the plush lime fabric beneath him. The tops of the carpet's threads seemed to brush underneath his ankle bone, they reached that high. Igor did not dare look down for that would mean looking away from the clay-coated bodies.

They remained still, nothing more than grey husks, or so he told himself as he neared the first one. A single fly buzzed lazily over the top of its back, circled, then landed on the nape of the corpse's neck. Every muscle in Igor's body tensed as he waited for the corpse to leap at him. It didn't.

This close, however, he recognised the man on the floor—even though his face was buried in carpet. His name had been Boris; a young lad who'd wanted nothing more than the honour of serving his country, always smiling with the naivety that comes with innocence and lack of experience. Igor remembered not seeing that smile much when the kid saw the battlefield, his brow puzzled, eyes wandering over the expanse of quagmire that extended all the way to the pale blue horizon.

He remembered feeling disappointed for the boy, knowing that whatever gallant dreams he'd had would be crushed by tomorrow when he led them into the fray.

'Not what you expected,' one of the other

men, Anatoly, had said, laughing and clapping the kid on the back. There was no humour in his voice, though. 'War isn't what they teach you in books and school.'

Igor could see the big soldier's body further down the hall, sprawled over the top of another. Again, he could not see the man's face as he lay on his front.

'There is no pageantry, no nobility—that's ivory tower thinking, made by the men that wage it so they can go to bed at night and sleep soundly while young boys like yourself dream of being heroes. What it's really about is those men getting to draw lines on a map while enjoying their new supply of whatever it is they've taken.'

'So what is that they want this time?' laughed another soldier; it sounded like a cry.

'Whatever the Ottomans have that we don't,' replied Anatoly simply.

The fly on Boris' neck buzzed, then settled. Igor was staring at it, his eyes huge and unblinking, as the memory flashed across his mind. Biting his bottom lip, he cautiously raised his left foot, aware of the muscles around his knee contracting and relaxing to perform this action, extending it over Boris' dead body until his boot settled into the carpet on the other side.

It was here that he felt exposed, his legs in a *V*-shape above the deceased, the rank odour rising from them seemingly intensifying until Igor tasted bile, his eyes watering, nostrils stinging. Rushing, he pulled his right foot over Boris.

Next was the huge body of Anatoly, heaped atop someone that Alex couldn't make out; they occupied the left-hand side of the hall, leaving a small gap on the right. Igor navigated this by side-stepping along with his back against the wall, aware that he was coming to a point where its blue surface was interrupted by doors, their wood an ornate, dark brown. He was past the bodies, hoping to try the doors in case they offered some escape from the stinking abattoir of a corridor, when something slumped behind him. It was a heavy sound, like something falling onto the carpet, that froze him.

The sweat-slicked skin of his spine itched as he sensed more movement behind him, movement that he knew without turning would be shambling. Another sound resonated, that of fingernails being dragged through carpet.

The upper half of Igor's body turned; the

steel that had been in his belly seemed to have spread into his lower half, cementing his legs. As he turned he heard a soft moan, mournful and forlorn, that made him squeeze his eyelids shut. They ripped open as five sets of nails latched into the flesh of his leg above the ankle.

A scream ejected out of him.

'You abandoned us,' cried the dead thing that had once been Boris.

Its flesh had a green tinge beneath its muck coating; it glared accusingly up at him from the floor with eyes like black marbles. It had crawled to him, legs dragged out behind it, useless. Igor couldn't breathe—it was like an invisible force had seized his chest—as the creature's nails dug further into the flesh of his leg.

'You led us to our doom and then you fled like a whimpering coward,' cried the monster at his feet. Its voice was a guttural croak.

He felt movement all around, shambling motions as the bodies reanimated, picking themselves up from the floor, boxing him in. Igor had to discern all of this from his peripheral vision, because his sight hadn't left the dead face of his former comrade, a man who had trusted him to lead them into battle and bring them out the other side, who now had a piece of his right temple missing, revealing the black skull and grey, wrinkled flesh of his brain inside.

'You belong with us, should have died with us.'

Igor twisted his eyes away, seeing the grey, prodding bodies of his troops walling him in and then the door on his right. He lunged for it, dragging Boris with him until the soldier's nails ripped from his leg, his slick hands fumbling with the doorknob. His lunge put him off balance, and he fell through the doorway without choice as it opened.

2

Alex woke to a sharp throbbing at the back of his skull and a knife pressed against his throat. The hand that held it belonged to Luka Ivanov; the elderly Baron sat over him, the sooty caterpillars of his eyebrows furrowed together.

'Start talking,' he said.

Alex registered that he was lying on what felt like a sofa, that the Baron's dark brown eyes were observing him with consideration and that the blade lay beneath his Adam's apple between the scruff of his beard hair. Blinking against the pain that radiated from the back of his head all the way to the hinge of his jaw, he understood from the Baron's eyes that the man would not hesitate to kill him.

'You didn't need to do that,' said Alex,

rubbing his injured skull. 'I'm not the one you should be afraid of.'

'After everything that's happened, I vehemently disagree. Now start talking, or I'll start cutting,' said Luka.

'Grandfather,' said a voice behind the Baron.

Over his shoulder, looking down at him, was Carla, eyes filled with reproach. The young version of Michael Volkov stood closer, brow glossed in sweat from his flight through the house, his gaze fearful and hard. Alex disregarded both of them in noticing the presence of the man whose arm was encircled around Carla's waist.

'He shouldn't be here,' said Alex, trying to rise.

'Steady.'

Luka had placed a hand on his chest, keeping him down while holding the blade close to his skin. Alex couldn't see it, but he could tell that he was bleeding.

'Why are you here?'

The panic in his voice must have struck those in the room, because all eyes turned to the newcomer. 'I got a note from Carla to follow everyone here; she said she was afraid. I climbed inside through one of the windows over there when I heard screaming from outside.'

At the words of the young man, Michael strode to the room's far right-hand side, moving around two snooker tables, their emerald-furred subjects bright beneath lantern light, to the windows there. Alex could hear him grunting as he attempted to open them, finding each one locked.

'I never sent you a note,' Carla said, turning to the newcomer; to the young Alexander Nicholai.

'No, the house did,' sighed Alex, his guts twisting with betrayal.

'Explain,' ordered Luka, pressing the knife to him.

'This place is alive, and it aims to feed off of all of you.'

Igor landed with a splat in something cold and soupy. Mud. That same grey mire that had swallowed his troops when he'd ordered them into a battle that turned out to be an ambush; one that his superiors had known was coming but had decided to trigger anyway with the intention of countering. Igor had overhead this the night before and had still obeyed their orders, yet when the blood had started to fly and his men's screams shook the air he had fallen back, observing the carnage as his men were slaughtered.

'Fuck,' he shrieked, arming the glop out of his eyes.

Mud caked his front, clogging his nostrils so that he was breathing it in. The slime hit the back of his throat and caused his stomach to upheave its contents in a jet before him, his mouth burning as it did. Palms planted in the mire on either side of the yellow puddle he had created, Igor breathed deeply, trying to regain some control over a mental state that felt like wet paper in his hands.

He had felt this way before, seeing his troops flung from their horses, their navy uniforms torn apart by gunfire and fountaining red. All memory of bravery, of honour had fled him, replaced with one primary instinct: flee. And he had done so—not just from the battlefield, but the war itself.

Now he had been brought back to it, it seemed.

The plain before him was a landscape of cratered muck as dark as tar, dead trees scorched black by fire; their branches were gnarled, skeletal fingers reaching toward the steel-grey sky. Flies buzzed incessantly. In the distance there was a sound like thunder, only Igor recognised it as cannon fire.

He whipped around, remembering the corridor of dead shambling things, and spotted the doorway that he had fallen through. It floated five feet above him, the ornate wooden door swinging wide so that the constant ochre light of the hallway poured out from the rectangular opening in the air. Igor could see the fur of the faded lime carpet, the swirls of silver in the pale blue walls, could even smell the spice of dust.

A glance around confirmed that the dead had not followed him through; nor could he spy them in the corridor. Stumbling to his feet, the muck sucking at his knees, he darted towards the door-shaped opening that hung in the sky. Just as he reached out, the heavy door snapped shut with a squeal of its hinges, its closing sounding as final as that of a coffin lid.

'No,' he yelled, fingers scrabbling against the wood.

It did no good; he could only touch the bottom section of the door, and even as he did it was fading from existence. The brown wood faded to grey, then seemed to drain away like an image in a photograph that had been exposed too long to the elements.

A banshee wind howled, ruffling his clothes and hair as he dropped to his knees, sobs retching from his chest. Igor didn't know how long he knelt there crying until the muck bubbled—it could have been hours or seconds—only that when a belch erupted out of the earth, he found himself staring into

Boris' black marble eyes.

He knew it was Boris on account of the missing section of the man's right temple; he also knew, even though the lower half of the man's face was submerged beneath the mud, that he was smiling. This proved true as the mushroom-white dome of Boris' head seemed to elevate out of the mire, revealing teeth like black tombstones.

'You're home,' crooned the corpse of the young soldier, his marble eyes rolling in ecstasy.

Igor could smell him now, a sickly mix like overly ripe oranges.

Heads were emerging from the sludge, rising in the same way Boris had, their skin just as white and flecked with dirt. They encircled him.

Igor scuttled away on his hands and heels, spraying muck, panting, until his back struck something. Craning his head up, he saw that it was one of the dead trees.

'What is it you used to say?' called Boris' voice, oozing dark delight. 'A company is nothing without its captain; you never knew how true those words were. You complete us.'

The dead thing's shoulders were free now,

and some of the others were close.

'We have waited, longing for you.'

Boris wiggled his arms free, casting vast spats of muck into the air. His fingers dug grooves into the earth as he scrabbled free, crawling with eel-like speed to grip Igor's ankles.

'Come join us in the mire,' he said, dragging Igor back into the circle that now consisted of reaching arms and hooking fingers. 'You'll like it, it's peaceful.'

Those hooking fingers were on him like a dozen skittering insects. Two forced themselves into his mouth and ripped away a flap of his cheek, leaving him screaming. Others found his eyes and buried in, popping their jelly. The rest tugged at his clothes, searching for flesh to scarp at as they swarmed on top of him.

CHAPTER **ELEVEN**

'Would you like to elaborate on that?' said Luka.

Gone was the fragile man at the end of his life that Alex had seen earlier; now there was a lethal glint in his dark eyes that bought vibrancy to his aged face. Alex had never exchanged a word with Luka Ivanov when he had been alive, but seeing him now he believed the tales told down at the tavern, of him slaying the mighty *Ruskak*, a giant bear with paws twice as big as a man's head that had haunted the forests of Tula in the years before he had been born.

'If you would permit me to sit up, I'll speak,' said Alex.

Luka stared at him, eyes like dark jewels behind the curtains of his silver mane.

'Grandfather, I think we can trust him,'

said Carla.

'This man urged on the death of your father. Why would you think that?' asked the Baron without taking his eyes off Alex.

'Because father is dead, because I think he's achieved what he wanted to achieve— and because I feel like I know him, don't you?'

This caused her grandfather to lean back, removing the knife ever so slightly.

'Was my son really conspiring to have me killed?' asked the Baron, pressing the knife once more against his neck.

'Yes, your son was a selfish, cruel fiend who craved power and hated seeing you give it away by treating those below you fairly,' said Alex without fear. 'He conspired with Heya to have you killed, enlisting Volkov's help with the promise of your granddaughter's hand in marriage. That way if Volkov got caught doing the deed they could deny everything, and Volkov was more than happy to play the part. He may come across as having noble blood, but there's nothing but mud in his veins. He's a con artist.'

The Baron seemed to peer into him, his fingers rotating the knife by the handle as he pondered. 'A father knows his son, even if he's unwilling to admit it,' he said eventually.

The Baron heaved himself to the far side of the sofa, allowing Alex to sit up. The room they were in was long, with low ceilings furnished in the same ornate mahogany as the rest of the house. A fireplace dominated its left-hand side with tall, rectangular windows on the right; arranged in the centre was a line of snooker tables.

'They're all locked,' said Michael Volkov who, having been so focused on trying to open windows, had not heard a word of what was being said.

His eyes were on Alex the younger with barely contained panic.

'Which one did you come through? Why did you close it behind you?'

'I didn't close it,' replied Alex the younger, taking in the windows.

'It's the house,' the elder said, finding all eyes on him. 'The house doesn't want us to leave.'

'I believe you were about to tell us something about that,' said Luka, his voice morose, yet firm.

'I'm sorry about Tomac,' Alex replied.

'No, you're not.'

'For you and Carla I am. Your son hurt me; he would have hurt a lot more people if I hadn't invited you all here. I will not feel remorse for that.'

'If what you say is true, then my father was an evil man,' said Carla Ivanov, stepping forward. Her pale skin was near luminous in the dim light of the room. 'What type of a man are you? A vindictive one certainly—one out for revenge, that is clear. The more important question is: *who* are you?'

Strings swelled from the western corner of the ballroom, producing a sweet, taunting sound. Dancers drifted over the polished oak floor, illuminated by three huge crystal chandeliers shedding golden light, their faces hidden behind Venetian masks. They rotated around the circumference of the dance floor, somehow magically in sync with the music and each other. Swaying in the eye of this whirling movement were two individuals, the only ones without masks, their laughter tumultuous.

'Heya, you're so bad,' scolded Brania, giggling.

'I'm just honest and you know it,' Heya replied, then hiccupped. The champagne they had drunk before she'd ushered them onto the dance floor was making her head spin on a different trajectory than that which her body was moving in.

'And fearless,' said Brania.

The gentleness of her tone, the way her brown eyes seemed to reach out and hold hers, made Heya consider the woman in her arms more carefully, her heart seeming to rise to her throat, its beat fluttering out of rhythm.

'Hardly,' she replied, feeling something not common to her emotional experience: bashfulness. 'I just say it how it is; can you imagine my Tomac...' the name echoed in diminishing recalls in her head, 'and your husband attempting to run the household if we suddenly left one day? It would be chaos.'

'Kazimir doesn't even know where his washed clothes come from. I imagine sometimes that he thinks he puts them into a basket dirty and that by magic they end up in his wardrobe clean,' said Brania, a hint of sorrow in her good-humoured voice. 'Do you ever wonder what it would be like?'

Her voice was tentative, afraid. It pulled Heya's eyes, which had been roaming the many bodies on all four sides of the vast ballroom that were either watching the dancing partners or in conversation with each other, back to the heart-shaped face of the woman opposite her. 'I'm sorry?'

'Running away together. Do you ever wonder what it would be like?'

There was apprehension in Brania's eyes of a sort that made Heya understand that uttering those words had taken a lot of courage. Neither of them had discussed what it was between them that caused them to be drawn to one another, why they promised themselves wordlessly after each secret rendezvous, usually when the rest of Tula's high society were occupied at events like the current one, that it would be the last.

It was just a silly game, Heya had thought once, her frosty disposition reaffirmed by the fact she hadn't even looked back at Brania lying on her and Tomac's marital bed, her chestnut hair tousled and undone around cheeks flushed red, watching her leave the room with wide eyes, horrified in their disappointment.

Yet, she could not quit that silly game.

Despite that, neither ever talked about it; they always found each other in quiet, shadow-veiled halls far away from others. There had been one time, when Heya had spotted Brania, wicker basket swinging from the crook of an arm, heading into the forest from a window in her castle. She had stalked her to some blackberry bushes she was picking from while humming some musical tune. After Heya had announced her presence, she feed Brania blackberries with a hand stained purple with their juices, while her other hand had explored the woman's body having stripped it bare. She still remembered the fevered frenzy that had overcome her mind, a volcanic wave that drowned all thought of danger or loyalty to her husband; it had hummed in her flesh, strobing with lightning flashes of fear and excitement. In the end she had licked the fingers of both hands, tasting blackberries, saliva and the salt from between Brania's legs as she lay on a bed of grass, her pale chest, the colour of fresh milk, heaving below.

Had she ever allowed herself to imagine running away with this woman?

The answer was no; her frostiness, like the stone walls of an impenetrable fort, prevented her from thinking such things, but as Brania's question resonated, becoming a sunrise inside Heya, she knew what she wanted. Wanted in the way her body wanted oxygen after being deprived of it. There was no questioning, no doubting, just absolute need.

'I would love that,' she said, and she saw a future without schemes, without the scrap and claw of social advancement; instead, there was contentment and freedom. A freedom to explore whatever this was between Brania and her. She saw the same in the heart-shaped face opposite hers as it lit up, eyes blazing, cheeks glowing.

Heya's last spoken word echoed as she twirled with Brania; like before it diminished in volume, yet as it did it seemed to transform, becoming her husband's name. Unlike before, however, it did not sound only in her head.

She glanced around, her brow creasing in a frown.

'What's wrong?' asked Brania.

Heya paused, still gazing at their surroundings, the frown remaining on her brow. 'Do you remember how we got here?'

This time it was Brania's turn to look, and as she did Heya begun to realise that what the string orchestra was playing was no longer sweet, it was deep-throated; a mounting, screeching rhythm that filled her with dread. So did the faces of the crowd, hidden behind porcelain masks of various designs: some glinted with gold, others were sketched with swirling ink lines. These masks did not just cover the eyes of their wearers, but obscured them from the fringe to the chin.

'No, I don't... and I don't remember ever being in such a place before,' said Brania.

The one thing each mask had in common, Heya noted, was the eyeholes; they were all like round pits of inky darkness.

The two women did another twirl, providing them with a panoramic view of the ballroom, and they saw that on its southern side were three huge windows of arched glass, allowing in the navy-coloured night. They held the same view they had seen earlier, one of Tula wrapped in blackness from a high mountaintop range. As they spun, both heard the sound of voices whispering, '*Tomac, Tomac*,' repeatedly, like a hushed chant.

'Nor do I,' Heya whispered.

A shuddering squeal erupted from the orchestra as bows scratched to a halt across strings. The dancers ceased their kaleidoscopic twirling. The clink of glasses and dull murmur of conversation faded into silence. All eyes were on them, staring.

'What's wrong with their eyes, Heya?' asked Brania, terrified.

The slow crawl of dread, like knuckles digging into Heya's spine, cleared any sense of drunkenness she had been feeling as her head whipped around. Now that all those eyes were upon them, she noticed it too: the people in the ballroom weren't wearing masks at all; their eyes were pools of inky blackness that wept down porcelain skin shining in the golden light raining from above. Their lips were thin slits in their faces.

A hand clamped down on Heya's bicep, ripping her from Brania's grasp. It belonged to one of the creatures, or so she initially thought as an overwhelming scent of oil invaded her nostrils. It cast off its face, along with a wig of black curls.

At first Heya thought it had indeed pried the porcelain skin from its flesh, for the face that grinned back at her was red. Then she recognised it.

'Tomac,' she said, her heart skipping in her chest.

His grin seemed to grow, revealing a line of teeth that were too white. These appeared whiter in contrast to the redness smeared across his cheeks and brow that looked to Heya to have a similar consistency as strawberry jam. 'Tomac, what happened to you?' she gasped.

'Oh, nothing that concerns you, darling. Just went for a little dip.' His voice was manic and jubilant, the grin splitting his face never diminishing.

Behind him, she saw the creatures beginning to sway toward them, their gait nonchalant and all the more ominous for it. Her husband still held her by the bicep, his fingers pinching hard enough to hurt.

'What you should be concerned about is this little display you two have going on,' he said, casting his leering gaze at Brania, who stood petrified.

'It was nothing,' she shot back, trying to twist out of his grip. She couldn't; his fingers were like steel.

'Now, now, don't try and lie to me. Do you really think I haven't seen you two? The looks, the constant sneaking off to indulge in deviant behaviour.'

'We've done nothing wrong,' cried Brania.

'Silence,' shouted Tomac, his voice echoing in the vast space.

Heya looked to Brania as the creatures

grasped her arms, saw the look of utter devastation on her face and felt powerless. More hands gripped her as well as Tomac let go, stepping back, his crimson face heinous. One of the creatures handed him a branch of wood, its end aflame.

'You know what the punishment is for deviants,' he told her.

The creatures swung both of them around, pointing them toward the fireplace, a giant alcove in the northern wall made entirely of white marble. Before it, reaching almost to the ceiling, were two stakes of wood, their lower halves draped with kindling.

'To burn,' his voice said from behind her.

The creatures begin to push them forward without a word. Heya heard Brania scream, 'No,' and knew there were tears in her eyes, she smelt camphene—or something like it— stronger than before and it made her dizzy as she tried to plant her feet. Her shoes slid on the polished floor of the ballroom as the muscles of her lower legs strained to find a grip and suddenly the red-faced man that was her husband was before her, in front of the left pyre. Brania screamed as she attempted to kick out against her captors; they just lifted her off the ground, legs cycling beneath her, and marched for the right pyre.

'You made me look like a fool,' said the red-faced man, staring into her eyes. His voice was solemn.

The maniacal grin, one that seemed as painted on as the blood, slumped as his eyes dipped to the floor, their gaze internal and woeful. Seeing him like that was a spear to Heya's gut, one that ignited fury in her, the same old fury used to maintain her frosty detachment for others, one built from a lifetime of always being dismissed on account of one thing and one thing only. She looked in his face, the fury filling her veins not with ice but fire, and saw that his motivation had nothing to do with Brania and her; it was all about him, and that made her burn with hate.

'Honey, you do a good job of that alone,' she spat.

As his head came rocketing up, she lashed out with her left leg, bringing it up between his legs and kicking him hard in the balls. A small yelp escaped him as his body jumped then sagged; the creatures, stunned by this action, loosened their grip enough that she could elbow free and pull the flaming torch from the red-faced man's hand.

As their fingers raked at the back of her dress she spun, the flame becoming a wheel of fire, and stabbed out with the torch. The creatures' cream suits caught in a whoop of fire, beginning at the lapels then spreading into both figures, lanterns of flame stumbling into the press of bodies surrounding them, igniting more. Panic overtook them, sending them fleeing in all directions as the ballroom filled with smoke.

The red-faced man seized at the bottom of her dress, his expression a snarl of hatred. She kicked his chin hard enough that his jaw snapped closed, tugged the dress from his grip, and marched towards Brania who in the panic had been abandoned by captors and watched with an open mouth.

Heya, grasping the woman above her hips, yanked her forward, kissing her heartedly as the room burned. When they separated, she said, 'Let's try that running away now.'

CHAPTER **TWELVE**

As Alex opened his mouth to speak, his throat locked by the blue eyes—his own—staring into him, something thumped at the rear of the room. It came from underneath the last snooker table.

'What was that?' asked Michael.

'We need to get out of here,' ordered Alex.

The *thump* came again, knocking the table out of alignment with the rest and making them all flinch. Whatever it was that lurked in the shadow beneath it was strong to be able to move such a heavy table.

The group were already backing toward the exit behind them, all eyes on the end of the long room, when whatever it was vocalised for the first time. Those that had grown up in the province of Tula knew what that yawning roar meant: *bear*. Yet none but one among them had heard one so deep, so disgruntled.

'It can't be,' whispered Luka.

Alex glanced at the Baron holding the thin knife and that saw the initials *K.S.* were stamped on it. His face was deathly pale, his eyes wide and fearful.

'What is it, Grandfather?'

A paw, the fur thick and matted with mud, reached out from the darkness behind the last snooker table. Its claws, dagger-long and yellow, raked the rich green felt, leaving five long gashes. The size of the paw alone caused the name to spill out of Alex's mouth: '*Ruskak*.'

As soon as he spoke, something massive erupted from the darkness, its dirty pelt causing it to blend in with the shadows of the dimly lit space as it tossed the snooker table aside like it weighed nothing. The table slammed into one of the windows with a crash of glass and clatter of wood. None of the group wanted to wait around to see what it did to the rest as the shadow-draped behemoth charged along the low-ceilinged room, slamming the door behind them as they left.

'How do we kill it? The house, I mean,' shouted his younger self as they fled down the corridor.

'How can we, if it's what the old man says it is?' snapped back Michael. 'Better to focus on getting out than being a hero; this isn't some fairy-tale.'

'Yes, *you* can,' said Luka Ivanov, taking the words right out of Alex's mouth.

Alex looked at the older man sprinting beside him; for someone in their seventies, he was surprisingly limber and swift on his feet. Again, he was reminded of the lethal glint in his eyes. 'I've killed things like this before,' he said.

They all fell silent at that, just in time to hear the door to the snooker room splinter apart. Ruskak, the bear that haunted the dreams of many of Tula's people, roared, seeming to make the very walls on either side of them vibrate. The lighter blue of the corridor allowed the group to see the giant beast in detail; its brown pelt was filthy and scarred with numerous white rake marks, particularly along its snout.

'Well, do you have any ideas now?' shouted Michael.

The beast's shoulders scraped along the walls of the corridor as it loped after them, its mouth spraying saliva, its yellowed teeth on display.

'We can hurt it... the house,' Alex said between gasps. 'It's a living thing... we're just inside it.'

'What does that even mean?' snapped Michael.

'It controls everything inside itself, except what we do,' Alex bit back. 'With us, it can only influence. So if we damage something, it stays damaged. I figured it out when I accidentally tripped and caused a mirror to fall; it shattered into pieces. Bad luck, I know, but the house... it was enraged with me for it.'

This was true: appearing to him as Carla, it had yelled through gritted teeth, 'Will you be careful?!'

The group sprang around a right turn and found themselves stumbling onto a forest path between trees as thick as horse carts, their trunks silver, stretching up into the heavens then branching out, their leaves creating a canvas of navy. They skidded off of the green carpet of the house onto a gravel path of silver that wound through these huge giants, disappearing into navy gloom. That same gloom existed between the trees to their left and right where the walls of the corridor had been. The only illumination seemed to radiate from the trunks closest to the path, their silver bark glittering diamond-like, as if they contained a luminescent sap.

It was clear to even those new to the house's manipulative ways that something was wrong; a tail of black smoke floated over the gravel pathway. Alex observed Luka sniffing at the acidic odour in the air. He glanced around, finding his younger self doing the same, peering back into the square portal in the air that led back into the labyrinthine maze of hallways. There was no sign of the bear.

'It looks like someone has already hurt it,' said Carla.

In the distance at the end of the trail, an orange light flared.

3

The walls groaned in agony as they flew down hallways clouded in smoke, coughing as it coated their tongues, their throats. The fire, unseen, boiled behind wood and carpet and stone; it was in the air they breathed, a desert-dry heat that devoured moisture. They each felt it press like a hot palm against their temples, or at their backs as they ran, skirts becoming charred tails around their legs.

'What do we do?' cried Brania, bending over as a hacking cough took hold.

Heya patted her back, staring at the T-junction that they had come to; the very air seemed lit with orange. Brania spat onto the floor as her fit subsided.

'We need to get out of here... come with me,' Heya said, taking her by the hand and leading her into the closest room, a small, sparsely decorated bedroom the likes of which a servant would have. The air wasn't as choked in here, the space cooler, and wanting to preserve it she closed the door behind her. 'We must be on the top floor.'

'How? We never came to any stairs,' said Brania.

From her tone, Heya guessed the woman didn't actually want her to answer. She had none to give; like Brania, she supposed she remembered running into darkness then suddenly finding herself in a ballroom filled with those monsters.

'Can you hear that?' Heya asked. Striding forward, not waiting for a reply, she crossed the room to the closed door opposite the room's entrance. Turning the doorknob and shoving it aside, the glorious sound she had heard increased in volume, bringing a smile to her lips. Rain hailed upon a small, rectangle window above the bathroom's toilet.

'Looks like we've found our way out,' she said to Brania, whose jubilant expression echoed Heya's own.

From outside the servant quarters came an agonised rending of wood.

'Come on, you're first.'

Brania had to step onto the toilet bowl to reach the tiny window's latch, which resisted at first then depressed with a squeal of metal, the glass swinging wide. Heya could smell the rain, falling so hard that it kicked up dirt on the roof, and thought she had never smelt such an exquisite scent in all her life. White lightning forked through the tumultuous heavens above, churning like a storming sea of ebony as Brania climbed from the toilet to the windowsill then squeezed out, skirt ripping on the window frame onto the roof. Heya made to follow, using the toilet as a step to the sill. When she went to pull herself through, fingers gripping the peeling frame of the window, she lifted her left leg off the toilet seat—only to feel a hand enclose around her ankle.

'You're quiet,' said Luka.

'Huh?' Alex's gaze snapped from the navy gloom beyond the border of the silver trail to the Baron on his left. The man was studying him, his grey eyebrows connected in a frown that darkened the sockets of his eyes. 'We're all quiet,' Alex replied, which was true.

The group was traversing the path in complete silence, staring to either side in expectation of an assault. The bear that had chased them had not—so far—reappeared.

'Does your first response to everything have to be bathed in sarcasm? Of course we are all quiet, because we are all thinking. My asking you such a question is to provide you the opportunity to share what exactly is on your mind. Which has merit, as you seem to be the most knowledgeable about our current predicament.'

Even with his condescending tone, Alex couldn't help liking the man. 'What I'm thinking is… something's wrong,' he answered.

'How so?'

'We should be dead. That bear should have run us down; it would have been easy for a thing like that on this trail, wouldn't you agree?

'I would,' replied Luka, nodding.

'It would have caught some of us, killed them, and forced the rest into whatever the hell that gloom is out there. The fact that we haven't, combined with these… anomalies…'

Alex was referring to a section on their left, where the hallucinatory illusion of the forest trail seemed to have broken down: instead of the continuing view into the woods was a stripe of familiar hallway wall, its navy sides faded.

The group trudged past it, their feet crunching on the gravel; even that didn't sound right to Alex's ears anymore. For one, the noise of their footfalls sounded delayed, as if the crunch made by their feet had to travel through honey to get to their ears. When it did, it was dull somehow.

'It tells me that something is wrong. Plus, there's the smoke, the sound.'

'I've noticed the sound,' said Carla, 'have either of you noticed the smell?'

Both Alex and Luka blinked at her, then without thinking raised their noses. They smelt the smoke first: it was as sooty and cloying as ever; underneath it however, the piney scent of the woods around them was barely noticeable. It wasn't that the smoke suffocated it—more like there was just less of it to smell.

'You can't think of this house as a building, you have to think of it as a person. An insane, diabolical person, for that matter,' Alex told them.

'That sounds insane,' shot Michael, irritated.

'It's not, not when you've been trapped inside it for as long as I have. Most of what it said to me was pantomime I'm sure; still, I got a sense of its personality. It is mad, but also petty, quick to anger and lust for revenge, much like a spoilt child.'

'How exactly did you learn this?' asked Carla, innocently.

'The walls told him,' said Michael, snidely.

'The house can take on the form of

anything it wants, like that bear back there.'

'Ruskak,' added Luka, nodding.

'What form did it take with you?' asked his younger self.

Alex paused, his eyes falling inward, avoiding Carla.

'Someone I knew.'

Hearing the sorrow in the man's voice caused them all to pause. Luka regarded his granddaughter then, remembering what she had said about knowing the person who had invited them into this trap; and even though he could not recall who, he would be lying if he didn't admit there was a feeling of familiarity about this man.

But it was all too much of a mess for his mind to sort through now. His priority was on getting his granddaughter out; the rest could be dealt with later, like what exactly he planned on doing with this mystery man and with Michael Volkov.

'What's your point, other than we should all be dead?' he asked.

'My point is that we aren't dead, and I think that's because its distracted.'

Luka made to ask, 'What's so important about that?' and saw the weary look in the tall stranger's blue eyes as he gazed ahead to the withering orange light, the source of the black smoke. He was thinking, and for some reason Michael couldn't help but feel that it would be detrimental to them all to interrupt whatever he was mulling over.

'Distracted by what?' asked Carla, in that breezy way of hers.

'I think we're about to find out,' he said vaguely.

They were coming to the end of the forest path, which seemed to be transforming back into the navy threaded walls that they knew so well, only these ones didn't end in silver leaves but roses. Before them was a wide archway leading into a vast open space; the staircase room where Tomac Ivanov had met his demise. Across the hexagonal space, they saw as they stepped cautiously out onto the landing, was where the smoke was emitting from: the house was on fire.

They all had enough time to contemplate what that meant when the ceiling gave in.

5

'Did you really think it was over? That you could have gotten away from me?' yelled the red-faced man that had seized upon Heya's ankle.

She twisted on the sill, whirling from Brania's horrified expression as it was illuminated in a flash of lightning that cracked across the sky to a sneering grin of lunacy. Her husband's blood-smeared mask was weeping sweat from the flames, flames that had progressed to inside the low-ceilinged servants' quarters. Cinders danced like fireflies in the air behind Tomac, landing on the narrow single bed she could see through the bathroom door, causing the duvet to smoke.

'Leave me alone,' she yelled.

'Not a chance, not without taking your

medicine.'

She heard Brania scream her name as the red-faced man yanked her toward him, her fingers sanded by the window's peeling frame. She managed to hold on, just as the red-faced man raised his right hand above his head.

In it, he held a hatchet.

Realising his intention was to stretch out her left leg and swing the blade down upon it, Heya lashed out with her right foot, connecting with his face. His hand immediately released her ankle, which she retracted as he clutched at his face with both hands screaming. Fresh blood, his blood, poured through his fingers.

'You fucking bitch!' he shrieked at her.

The cage of his fingers fell away, revealing a blood-spewing hole just below his right eye. It had been made by the heel of her shoe; Heya had felt it pierce his greasy skin when she'd jabbed out with her foot, the sinking sensation briefly terrifying her more than anything. He's got me, she'd thought, as his flesh pulled at her like living quicksand.

The thought of it was like being struck by lightning; she skittered backward, palms pulling, butt-shuffling over the windowsill onto the flooding roof of the house. Hands gripped her shoulders, helping her up. She was already drenched by the torrential rain, which robbed her body not just of its warmth but her sight.

The window was now a black maw as rainwater continued to strike her eyelids, forcing her to blink rapidly. Heya lashed a forearm across her face, drying them enough to see the sneering red face of her maniacal husband as he hoisted himself through the window frame onto the roof. His hatchet was thankfully gone, dropped when the point of her heel had stabbed into his cheek.

'There's no need to be hysterical,' he explained to them. His voice was calm, teaching. 'It's just a disciplinary matter, over in a second. The same way it was when you dropped your mother's jam jar; remember telling me about that, Heya? Your mother told you to leave it alone, but you couldn't resist that tiny voice in the back of your head that wanted more. It's just like that, if you fight and flee, then longer this will be.'

'You're not him,' Heya said, her diaphragm hitching as grief contorted inside her.

'No?' said the red-faced thing, its bloody mask raining from its jaw as rain lashed upon it. 'How am I not? He was cruel and vicious and cared only for himself.'

Brania and Heya backed away as the thing stalked forward, backing them against a huge dome of stained glass that dominated the central space of the bleak rooftop that rose around them on all sides like ramps of slate tile. The world was a torrent of gushing water, whipping wind and thunder.

'Not just himself,' shouted Heya back. 'He cared for me.'

'Oh yes,' breathed the monster, gripping her bicep. 'The great and cruel Tomac had space in his dark heart for a creature as malicious and self-serving as him. You really think she and you can survive? What happens when she learns about the real you, not the one that picks her up and puts her down whenever she wants, but the one that will cut her throat if it means saving her own neck?'

'Shut up and leave us alone,' screamed Brania, moving forward.

As quick as a viper the creature struck out, slapping the back of his left hand across Brania's cheek, sending her plunging into the water pooling at their feet.

'Stay out of this,' it warned. Turning back to Heya, it said, 'We all need a little disciplining sometimes.' Then, as lightning stroked across the sky like a blade of light, it shoved her.

6

Those on the landing below ducked on reflex at the sound of shattering glass. A cloud of it, of glittering indigos, ruby, emerald and sapphire, sailed past them, accompanied by a wail that was all finality. The void of the hexagonal space swallowed it, pelting the carpeted floor fifty feet below as they looked up.

There, caught above the fall on a string of wire cables that twanged with her weight, bobbing up and down, was Heya, the charred and ruined tail of her dress dangling. She had landed on her back, golden hair a disarrayed halo around her head.

'Mama,' yelled Carla, gripping the landing banister.

If Heya had heard she made no move to look over her shoulder; instead she was fixed on the hole in the dome as rain poured through. Alex squinted, eyes struggling to pierce the darkness, then in a flash of lightning he saw what she was staring at.

'Impossible,' he breathed.

Leaping through the damaged section of the glass came Tomac Ivanov, landing on the balls of his feet on two of the crisscrossing cables. Once more Heya dipped and rose as the weight of him rippled outward; only this time a groan erupted from the walls they were nailed to.

'We need to do something,' said Carla, her voice a plea. 'We need to save them.'

It showed in her eyes, which showed too much white to Alex. It didn't matter that she hadn't figured out what he had already guessed—that it might not be either of her parents up there, that this was all a ploy by the house. He stood at the banister with her on his left, and to his utter despair he heard himself say:

'There's nothing we can do.'

7

For Heya, there was the sensation of her feet leaving the ground, of her legs becoming parallel with her torso, as she fell backward onto the dome. There was no pain as it shattered underneath, becoming a hailstorm of a thousand shimmering pieces plummeting alongside her. That came when she suddenly stopped falling, not because she had hit the ground—her senses relayed to her mind that there was still a vast void beneath—but because two spikes of brilliant pain erupted at her shoulders and to a lesser degree at her buttocks. These dipped with her weight, sounding like the world's biggest springs, then bobbed back into place.

She grabbed at whatever was cradling her, gripping it until her hands grew white, its touch oily. It ran the length of her spine. She could see the imitation of Tomac leering from the darkness outside as white light veined intermittently throughout. He leapt onto the wires nesting her, an axe materialising out of nowhere and into his hands, the tree chopping kind.

'I'm actually sad this is over, you know,' said the Tomac-thing, placing a hand over its heart. 'You make this so much fun, Heya.' Strands of drool stretched from either side of its mouth.

'Fuck you,' she shrieked at him, throat burning.

She couldn't do anything: if she let go of the cables to defend herself, she would slip to her death. She was trapped, helpless.

'Leave her alone!' screamed a voice that she recognised as her daughter's.

Heya craned her neck as much as she could, seeing Carla on the landing below with the others. The Tomac-thing produced a laugh that sounded like a swarm of buzzing insects.

'Not so heartless anymore. Seriously, this is too rich,' it said.

8

The wail that the group on the landing had heard did not belong to Heya but Brania, having just witnessed the woman she loved pushed to her death. Her cheek stung from the slap administered by the monster that had pushed her. Rainwater continued to hail but, through the onslaught, she observed that same monster wink at her, his lips smirking in delight, before propelling himself after her beloved.

Stumbling, Brania rose, skin frozen by the icy downpour and prickling, staggering to the hole in the dome's surface. She didn't know what she felt in that moment—there was no air left in her lungs from her wailing, and the numbing effect of the water seemed to have invaded the flesh beneath—but an unreal sense, a disbelief so great it stripped her from the reality of the moment, of losing Heya.

She peered through the broken dome.

'Heya,' she breathed.

Warmth flooded out from her heart at seeing the woman alive, lying on the cables below. That warmth ignited and became fire as her eyes rounded on the monster clutching the axe.

Images, fragmented and dazzling like shards of a mirror, cycled in her mind. She saw Heya kicking the monster's balls with a gritted expression; she saw her fingers, stained with blackberries, reaching out to her and recalled their sweet taste as they slipped into her mouth, Heya's eyes closed, dozing beneath a blanket of rose-coloured furs, one pale shoulder exposed as she rested. There were others, hundreds that came without any thought or contemplation, just the impulse to act.

9

The group was so transfixed by what was happening above that none of them had noticed Brania Maca until she was plunging through the air, arms outstretched, fingers splayed into claws and aimed straight at Tomac. What was even more surprising to those that knew her was the expression of utter hatred on her face as she coiled around him as he made to swing the axe, forcing him off balance.

They watched as he teetered to the left, cables shrieking, as her legs whipped around within the bell of her dress, becoming an anchor. There perhaps would have been a chance of him shrugging Brania off if not for those legs, their weight causing the cables to rupture from the walls, showering stone and dust. Those watching flinched, using the banister as cover, as Brania and Tomac separated in the air. Carla Ivanov watched, incapable of shying away, as she sailed downward, limbs circling, her face serene, joyous even while Tomac's was a sneer of rage.

She wanted to scream, 'Thank you,' for her mother was saved, clutching onto a cable that had come loose on one side, swinging over the landing they all stood on. She didn't, though; she was incapable of speech. She could only stare straight across the chasm at the centre of the room as it swallowed both plummeting figures. After some time one thump resonated from below.

There was no scream. Even the sound of Brania's body meeting the floor was dull, unimportant like the background noise in an old house with creaky boards. That knowledge reached into Carla and tugged, the insignificance of the sound, the last noise Brania would ever make; yet she was anything but insignificant.

CHAPTER **THIRTEEN**

'We need to get out... now!' said Alex.

The moans from behind the walls had increased as the flames progressed on the opposite side of the grand staircase. Black smoke pumped out from all three landings, turning the vast space into a chimney as it flowed out of the damaged dome. Meanwhile the ornate wood on the other side of the building had begun to blacken, erupting in points to become orifices of fire.

'Is this the only way down?' asked Heya, still covered in brick dust.

The group had helped her down by catching the loosened end of the cable she had held onto once it had swung over the landing. She stood, arms wrapped around Carla's shoulders, eyes damp with tears yet bright with determination.

'It's the only way I know. Quickly, let's climb down,' replied Alex.

Luka made to follow the group only to discover that Michael Volkov was not with him; he was lingering behind, gazing dreamily into the darkness of the surreal corridor that had portrayed itself as a forest path. He could still make out some of the silver-trunked trees in the hallway's gloom, only their appearance was faded, see-through.

'Michael,' he called.

The young man did not respond swiftly, despite Luka barking his name. Instead, his head did a slow wheel from the dark hallway to Luka's gaze, his expression vague.

'Huh,' he grunted.

'Come on man, this whole place is going up in flames. We have to leave.'

This seemed to reach him; the kid shook his head, eyelids fluttering, and Luka was pleased to see some sort of recognition return to his expression.

'What were you doing anyway?' he asked as Michael joined him in descending the staircase. The others were already on the second landing where the air was a firework display of swirling cinders.

'Nothing,' he muttered.

There were dark bags like purple bruises under his eyes, Luka noted with concern. His skin was sickly pale; even his lips had lost colour. He made to inquire further when a loud rending noise shrieked out from the staircase above. All turned in horror to see that the third-floor section where they had been was hanging free from the wall, its carpeted floor and banister ablaze. A series of wooden beams connected it still, but more rending came from them, a sound that Luka thought of as being a louder version of nails on a chalkboard.

The group watched as they snapped one after the other, sending the third-floor staircase tumbling forward. The landing section, which they had previously been standing upon, smashed into the one on the second floor where the rest of their group stood, destroying the banister and ripping half with it before crashing to the vast space below. Luka screamed, seeing the others disappear beneath the giant pyre, feeling hot air radiating from it as it sailed past.

'Carla, Heya,' he called, coughing on smoke.

'We're okay,' screamed back the voice of his daughter-in-law. 'Keep running.'

He did as he was told, Michael already sprinting ahead, vanishing into the veil of soot. Covering his mouth, Luka did his best to keep up, following the spiralling steps that coiled round the circumference of the strange room. It was only as he was descending the first-floor stairs that he could finally make out his family.

He saw his daughter-in-law stop short of the blaze that occupied the middle of the room, the wood of the staircase having transformed into a blazing bonfire. Carla stood at her side, holding her hand as she gazed into the heart of the flames.

Brania, thought Luka, knowing that she was paying respect to the woman that had saved her life, the woman whose body was now buried beneath the fire.

The others watched on from the doorless portal to the staircase room. In the second it took for him to glance at them his eyes were torn back as a scream erupted from both Heya and Carla; something was lurching out of the flames.

Luka, spying two swords hung on the staircase wall, their blades crossed, snatched one by its golden handle. He planted himself between his family and the flaming apparition marching at them, leaving a trail of fiery footprints in its wake. It was in the shape of a man, but it was featureless, its body made of molten fire.

'Go! Run! I'll occupy it,' snapped Luka.

It had been a long time since he'd held a sword—his arms seemed to have forgotten the weight of such things—still he held it upright, his feet apart. At the sound of his words the apparition transformed, its flaming hind darkening and becoming flesh as it moulded into the image of his dead son, smiling gleefully.

'Really, you'll occupy me,' it said, holding a similar sword in its own hand.

'Grandfather,' cried Carla's voice.

'Go, child!' he shouted back, affirming his feet.

'Such sentiment,' mocked the grinning creature.

Luka leapt forward, bringing the heavy sword down on what should have been its skull only for it to clang to a stop. The creature had whipped his own sword up to block the blow, moving with frightening ease and a speed that sapped whatever hope Luka had of winning this. Didn't matter anyway, he thought, he was buying time.

Heya, still holding her daughter by the hand, nodded at Luka and turned to flee, finding the young man called Michael that her husband had favoured in her way. His expression was one of joyful accomplishment.

'He said I could become master of the house,' he told her.

She looked down to where the pain branched out from and saw his hand, its fingers bloody, wrapped around the handle of a knife. Its blade had been thrust all the way to the hilt into her belly. From behind, she could hear the metallic clang of swords as her father-in-law fought to save them; she smelt smoke, tasted ash and felt the heat of the fire drawing beads of sweat on her brow as Michael withdrew his knife.

Her hands fumbled over the wound with little strength, blood spewing through her fingers as Carla screamed, 'No!' Heya's knees unhinged slowly and she folded to the floor. Carla dropped alongside her, clutching at her belly. Blood pooled in her lap.

'All of it,' said Michael, his voice and gaze somehow disconnected from the reality in front of him. 'He said I could have all of it.'

On hearing Carla's cry, Luka Ivanov

snapped his head around, providing the creature guised as his son the opportunity to slap its opponent's weapon from his hand. The sword spun off to the right, landing on the carpet close to Alex, who looked up in time to see the monster run his blade straight through The Good Baron. He watched in horror, dry-mouthed, as the sword pierced the elderly man's chest and exploded out of his back in a gout of gore, the silver blade made crimson by it.

Luka roared in anguish, not so much in pain, Alex believed, but in defeat, in not being able to keep the monster at bay. That monster gripped him by shoulder, hoisted him into the air, turning his sword into a spike.

'This is the best meal I've had in centuries,' it said to Luka.

Its voice was a mind-needling buzz of insect voices.

Even then the Baron was reaching for its false face, his fingers flexing like claws. It tossed him aside, catapulting his injured body from his sword until it struck the far wall.

Alex seized upon the sword at his feet, though his mind was dumb to the possibility of using it. Instead, flashing inside it were the words, 'I did this,' as he stared at the still body of Luka Ivanov, sheathed in dust from hitting the wall.

They were red, those words, as red as the rose designs surrounding them.

2

'Mama,' cried Carla into Heya's ear.

It sounded far off, as if she had spoken through water. Heya tried to look at her and found that the world had dimmed; even the fires streaking like orange veins down the walls were dull. Carla's face was a blur. Still, she could tell she was crying.

'Please don't... don't go.'

Heya heard another voice then, one that seemed to reflect the detached sense of feeling she felt right then. It didn't seem human, that detachment.

'It's everything I've ever wanted,' it said.

There was a motion in the dimming world as something possibly human blurred across her vision. This was Alex the younger tackling Michael as he made to slash at Carla with his knife.

She paid it no mind; all her concentration was on getting the image of her daughter's face to come into focus. Eventually it did, and she could see her tear-streaked, pinched expression, her skin dirtied by soot but pale beneath and oh so beautiful.

'I'm sorry,' she managed. 'I haven't really been the best mum, have I? It's not... it's nothing to do with you, I have never been prouder of anything than I am of you.'

The world was dimming, dimming to black, a black that seemed to wade in like a tide engulfing all of her surroundings until Carla's weeping face was all she saw.

'I love you,' she gasped.

3

Heya's head slumped against Carla's shoulders, eyes wide, seeing nothing. What fading strength she had evaporated, the hands clamped at her belly sagging.

Carla saw all this through a prism of tears.

Grief contorted her, strangling her throat of air. She sat on the carpeted floor, diaphragm working, cords bulging in her neck until suddenly whatever invisible creature held her grieving let loose, allowing a wail to explode from her; that wail, and her mother's presence, became the world for those next few seconds. No house, no fire existed, just unfathomable pain.

When it was done, when she could scream no more, Carla opened her tear-drowned eyes to see Michael Volkov on top of Alex, hands at his throat, squeezing until the young man she loved was turning cherry red. She spied Michael's knife, slick with blood, on the floor before her. Rage wormed within the muscles of her jaw; her body shook with it

Carla grabbed Michael by the forehead and shoved the knife into his back. His entire body went rigid, a gasp of air escaping him. She yanked it out only to stab it back in again and again and again until the rigidity left him and what she was stabbing felt like nothing more than a piece of meat from the butcher's.

Alex, freed and gasping, tossed Michael's body aside, his hands hesitating before hugging Carla to him. The young woman was speckled with scarlet, eyes wide and dazed as her chest heaved from the exertion.

'Thank you,' he whispered.

4

'Young people,' said the disguised creature, 'such emotion.'

It made to stride at the pair, only to halt as Alexander Nicholai stepped into its path, sword upraised, slate eyes gritted in their sockets by hate.

'I'm sick of hearing your patronising bullshit,' he said, spitting at its feet.

The false Tomac raised one of its black eyebrows. 'My, my, what happened to our pact?'

'Like you were ever going to honour it,' he answered.

'See... you know me so well,' it sighed.

Behind it, the burning pyre was creating a giant plume of acidic black smoke; it stung Alex's eyes and left his tongue coated in grit, but still he refused to take his gaze off the imitation in front of him. Clasping the sword with both hands he tried to mimic Luka's stance, his fury so great the muscles of his arms seemed to twang.

'Carla, Alex, head for the front door. I'll keep this thing distracted enough for you to get out,' he shouted while still facing forward.

The pair looked at him, still holding each other, their bodies weary.

'I know you, don't I,' yelled Carla over the agonised groans of the house.

'And I know you in another life,' he whispered to himself.

'Let's go,' said Alex the younger, taking her hand.

As the pair ran for the exit and into the hall where the front door resided, the imitation spoke: 'They'll never get out. No one gets out.'

This time it was Alex's turn to sneer.

'We'll see.' And with that he charged, yelling.

5

Once more the air rang with the clang of metal on metal as Carla and Alex staggered toward the front doors of the house. The groaning within the walls had risen to deafening levels and now the floor trembled as if experiencing an earthquake. They stumbled past the ticking grandfather clock, its glass front wrinkled with a spiderweb of cracks, and grabbed at the handles of the door. Neither could be moved.

'What do we do?' shouted Alex.

He was staring at the doors; now, they depicted images of the house itself on them.

'Is this the part where you get to be the hero?' hissed the creature through the V-shape their locked swords had made.

Alex stood, his own blade painfully close, as he threw all his weight forward against the thing that had offered him the chance of revenge. It sneered back at him, its lips peeled back far beyond that which was humanly possible to reveal red gums and rows of serrated teeth. Yet, it did not look well; its skin had a waxy sheen to it. It seemed as well to be sweating.

'Is it your chance to make up for all the damage you've done? Luring those people—half of whom were innocent—to me.'

Its breath was rancid, the reek of a diseased body that's begun to rot. The smell of it made him gag.

'No,' he said, straining against the creature's superior strength. 'It's my chance to give them a chance that I never had, to do something different.'

Alex moved fast, letting go of the sword's handle with one hand and striking through the V-shape made by their blades. His fist connected with the thing's nose, although it did not feel like one to his knuckles—it did not indent as flesh does but yielded like clay. Still, it caught it by surprise, causing it to stagger backward, trailing its sword with it.

'I know what you are now,' Alex shouted.

Not giving the apparition time to recover, he darted forward and lashed out with his blade at whatever he could. This turned out to be the back of the creature's knees, causing it to straighten up and let out a monstrous bellow of pain. Its face did not resemble anything close to human as it did, more a crude sculpture of wax.

Carla, who had been depressing one of the door handles with all her strength, fell forward as it finally gave, the door swinging wide. The pair, unable to move, stared at the outside with mouths agog, seeing Tula's lights in the distant gloom beyond the edge of the rocky plateau pelted by the rain. Holding hands, they charged forward, feeling the eyes of the house glaring upon them, until they leaped from the top step and landed on the rock of the mountain. Then it was gone.

They turned, already drenched, to stare at the three-storey structure, feeling nothing in their hammering hearts residing from it, even as the door snapped shut and both of them screamed. There was an impossibility about it as they recalled the labyrinth of space that existed inside it, which did not meet with its outside appearance. Yet even with these memories it did not seem evil to look at, nor did it seem filled with that smug type of maliciousness that they had heard echoing in its words when it had spoken to them. It seemed ordinary: boring, somehow.

Carla almost wanted to creep up its steps and rap on the door, just to see if it had all actually happened. Alex grabbed at her, saying, 'What are you doing?'

Angered, she wheeled to him, meaning to shout, when she suddenly realized she was a foot away from stepping onto the first stone step. She had no memory of ever having begun to walk toward it at all.

'I don't know,' she said, suddenly more afraid than she had ever been.

Light—not the soft, ochre light that had spilled from the building's windows earlier, but a brilliant rainbow of it—beamed out from them now alongside a low, humming noise that was increasing in volume.

'You're just like them, Tomac and Michael,' said Alex, panting heavily.

All he could taste and smell was soot and dry heat.

'You think you're something special, but you're not. You're petty and cruel, which makes you a small thing.'

'You bastard,' spat the creature, its nose misshapen now. 'They were mine.'

It stared at him with eyes as black as a doll's eyes.

'Not anymore,' replied Alex, feeling oddly relaxed.

The fire was still raging, the carpet splitting underfoot. Plaster and dust rained down from above while smoke continued to funnel upward.

'How long can you keep this up? Alex

asked. 'I know this must be hurting—you can control anything you like in here as long as it's based on our fears, but the house is you and you are the house so if it hurts, you do too—that's how it works, right?'

'You're not wrong,' it replied with utter loathing. 'But you're also never leaving this place.'

There was a noise from far above, that of glass breaking. Suddenly the smoke from the centre of the room was crushed flat underneath a waterfall of water—not rainwater, this was far too much to be coming from the outside world. Plus, like the blood that had drowned Tomac Ivanov, it stayed contained as if by some invisible barrier.

When it was done the fires were out, and there was no sign of water damage. The house was reverting back to how it had been when Alex had found it. Carpets were restitching themselves; walls were reconfiguring as if all the harm inflicted to them was somehow being done backward.

'I'm fine with that,' Alex replied to the guised creature.

The maw of its mouth curled with rage. Alex brought his sword up so the point was aimed at its head.

'I was a dead man long before I ever met you.'

The low humming noise increased to a continuous whine, rainbow light no longer beaming from the windows but the very stone and tile that made up the building, as Carla and Alex hugged each other, eyes closed against the brilliance. Just as their ears felt ready to explode it ceased, stopping completely. The house was gone, as if it had never been there before. The pair looked at the place where the building had stood; there was nothing that indicated anything had nestled against the craggy rocks that stabbed at the heavens.

'Is that... is that it? asked Alex.

'I think so,' said Carla, peering through the rain.

After some time, Alex asked, 'What do we do now?'

'Home,' she replied, 'we go home.'

ACKNOWLEDGEMENTS

This book and my participation in the Price Manor project would not have happened without some very special people, my Spooky Friends. Thank you to Thomas Gloom and Spencer Hamilton for creating our little group of horror fiends; even if Price Manor hadn't happened, I would be eternally grateful to be part of such a supportive network not just for writing, but life itself. Thank you to Mike Salt, the OG behind the whole thing, for believing I could be part of the Price Manor team. It was unbelievably validating to wake up (because I slept through the initial string of messages concerning this project) and discover I'd been chosen to be part of something that is so special. And Price Manor is special, not just as a set of stories but as a playground for creatives to come and hone their skills. Thank you to everyone in that group (in no particular order): Jay Alexander, Michael Goodwin, Mike Salt, Carla Elliot, Haley Newlin, Briana Morgan, Kyle Winkler, Thomas Gloom, Marcus Hawke, Spencer Hamilton, Kelly Brocklehurst, Sabrina Voerman, Kalvin Ellis, Jeremy Megargee, Christopher Badcock and Mona Kabbani.

ABOUT THE AUTHOR
JAMIE STEWART

Jamie Stewart is a horror author and editor. His books include *Price Manor: The House That Bleeds*, *I Hear the Clattering of the Keys (And Other Fever Dreams)*, and *Mr. Jones*. He has co-edited such anthologies as *Welcome to the Funhouse* for Blood Rites Horror and *The Sacrament*, coming this October from DarkLit Press. His short stories can be found in various anthologies, podcasts and YouTube channels.

Jamie lives in Northern Ireland with his wife and dogs, Poppy and Henry. He can be found on Instagram **@jamie.stewart.33** where he reviews and promotes books.

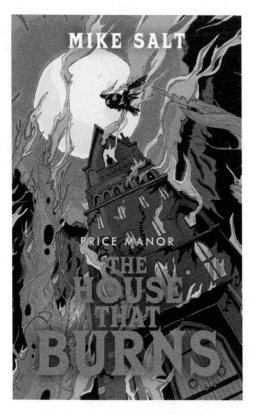

COMING MARCH 2022
THE HOUSE THAT FALLS
BOOK THREE IN THE **PRICE MANOR** SERIES

FROM **JAY ALEXANDER,** AUTHOR OF
**STARVING GROUNDS (COMING JUNE
2022)**

Printed in Great Britain
by Amazon